*Roots & Branches Series*

XXXXXXXXXXXXXXXXXXXXXXXXXXXXXXXXXXXXXXXXXXXXXXXXXXXXXXXXXXXXXXX

# Truth Truth Truth Truth

## SERGE GAVRONSKY

"I will not finish that sentence till I have made an observation upon
the strange state of affairs between the reader and myself…"
(Laurence Sterne, "Tristan Shandy" (NY: The Modern Library, n.d.)

"All this as true as it is true…"
(Thomas Mann, "Joseph and his Brother" (NY: Alfred A. Knopf, 1938)

XXXXXXXXXXXXXXXXXXXXXXXXXXXXXXXXXXXXXXXXXXXXXXXXXXXXXXXXXXXXX

SPUYTEN DUYVIL
*New York City*

ISBN 978-1-941550-61-8


Library of Congress Cataloging-in-Publication Data

Gavronsky, Serge.
[Poems. Selections.]
Truth truth truth / Serge Gavronsky.
pages ; cm
ISBN 978-1-941550-61-8
I. Title.
PS3557.A957A6 2015
811'.54--dc23

2015029820

TRUTH

# Truth in Berlin

## The Infiltration of Words

# Chapter I



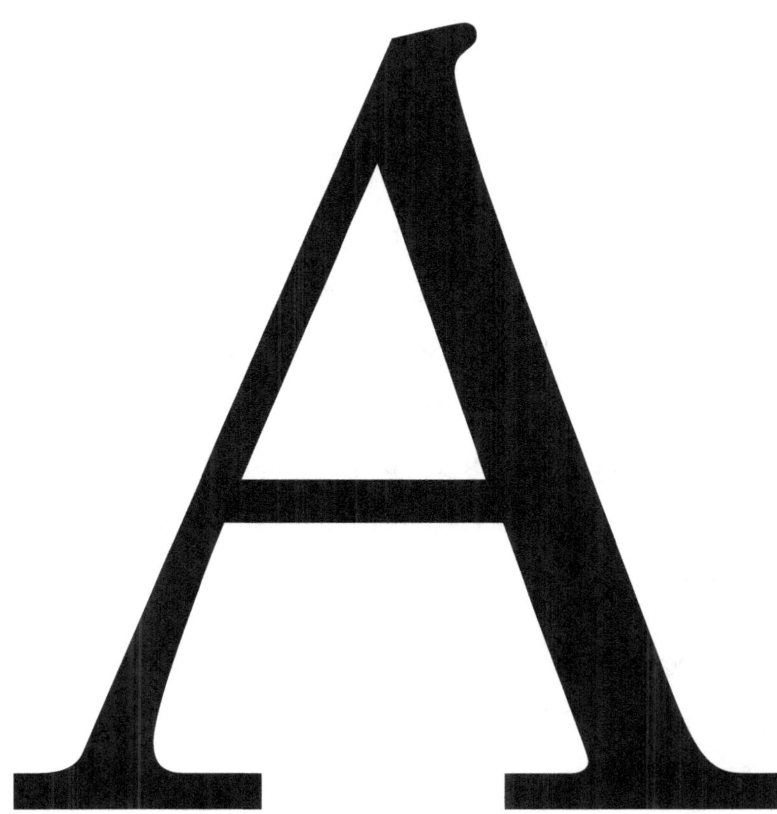

A Turkish prostitute walks down a Berlin sidewalk, caught in a large mirror behind the bar. Two men See her, elbows on the bar, and a large glass of beer in each of their right hands. The bartender Whispers: "I can tell you who she is, as do all the men who ask her where she comes from. What are her Fees How far away does she live? Is she alone, or does she have a pimp she's got to pay?" Their voices are inaudible. They can easily imagine her. They can identify her by her high heels, her tight black skirt, a Handbag, probably made in Estonia. If not so revealing. A  handbag, probably made in Estonia, if not,  Elsewhere by slaves or so poorly paid women workers, sewing all day and, when there's a fire, choking On death.

Windows closed.

Exists closed.

A mountain of handbags remain.

Meanwhile, Owners sun bathe on a foreign beach, perhaps in Florida where hidden money bought a Seashore property.

Sees herself in a large mirror behind the bartender.

They're all drinking Berliner Weiss. Soon, they'll be singing communist songs, learned at home in East Berlin.

The bartender leaps over the black bar with a baseball bat in his hands, a gift from a sentimental  American soldier who had given it to him, in exchange for a couple of beers. He swings it at an Estonian Unemployed migrant. A man falls, still holding his glass. The police cuff him, take away his baseball bat. The man on the floor: the police call for an ambulance. Tubes in his mouth. Handcuffed to the side of The bed. The nurse looks like King Kong. A Turkish prostitute looks on without glasses.

Two men, FATSO and SKINNY, remember a sex shop (for adults, only)  with a blond talking a mile a Second in the window display. She says: "Dildo Eilfel Tower, 34.90 euros. You can buy it either in blue or Pink.

And a Vaginal Stimulator."

Then, in the same window, the gorgeous blond says: " If you buy one, you'll get your first SEXTOY." (My Distant cousin, walking on upper Broadway, stops at 2795, and there, found three pornos in a plastic Bag 3 pornos and sent them to me. She spent $9.99.)

For some reason, FATSO momentarily went beyond the edges of the mirror. SKINNY stands in an Imitation mirror of some famous French painting.

Both look at her reflection.

She imagines what both are imagining.

Both salivated, memorizing the center fold of the famous Gutenberg for Adults, featuring nurses

Wearing transparent black undies.

Both assume she's a "nurse."

She come out of silence, and says: "I won! You cheated, both of you, with your mannered hands. I did Come, as I frequently do, with the shower head! What else? I come from a small village, 50 km east of Istanbul. I frequently, and without knowing it, return to my past.."

Both assumed she'd get on her knees.

"I RIDE MY BIKE to the Blue Mosque in 38 minutes. I stop outside an expensive rug dreamer who offers Me a small glass of apple tea, as they do everywhere else, especially in the souk. I don't have time to Wander around the Grand Bazar, looking for pair of shoes. How can anyone expect to find anything, When they say there're 60 lanes and 4000 shops!"

Both look ahead, dreamily participating in a group grope or, better still, posing in front of a large mirror.

Did she have friends?

Both neglect their Berliner Weiss. Both hope for an all-night gamble.

She imagines what both are imagining.

Later, she would clean herself in the toilet.

The following morning, she soaps herself again, then once again.

Laughter.

"Far from my village, my behind worn down from all that biking!"

Later, High Heels, along the sidewalk.

Smoking one of those foul, smelling, filtered German thing!

The image moves.

I saw one of myself on an opposite sidewalk. She looked like a 1936 female swimmer!

"Well, I know who I am.

Does she really know who she is?"

"You?"

 Both of us wore blue tee shirts, bought in a second hand-military store.

The bartender, his back to the mirror, asks if they had ever spent a night with a prostitute, right off a Berlin sidewalk ? He says there may be a problem from some eastern European country, maybe  Syphillis?

"Let me answer:

"An adventure is an adventure."

The mirror speaks in a foreign tongue, with a heavy eastern European accent.

I whisper:

"both of them are flabby, and why that haircut?"

She says: "How do you like it?"

Both look at each other and whisper: "How I wish I could speak her foreign language!"

"I wish I could, simultaneously, speak my own and hers!" Then he mumbles: "Could I live, simultaneously, In my language and hers?"

She stops.  Lights a stinking Eastern European filtered cigarette.

Both try to get out of the mirror.

She asks herself: "Did either of them ever fuck a stranger from an Eastern European country?"

They walk upstairs, behind her swaying ass, and dream.

She opens the door.

 No lights.

A couch, nearby. A bed, with a red cover. On the wall, an Eastern European poster of a circus.

She walks into the bar.

You can smell sweat.

"I'm the only woman. Clean. No sweat."

Now, a crowd cheers for their team on a soccer field: Milan vs Madrid.

Answer: "In a pool! It cost me 70 pfennigs. Cheap for a beginner." she adds: "just for you!"

In her apartment, they hear her pissing.

One of the two men says:

"Probably a stream of consciousness…Ha! Ha! Ha!"

She writes to her mother, in her new German: "Liebe Mutti,

Last week I bought new clothing! A New Coat for the cold winter in Berlin, and New Shoes!" She adds: "I Have a four week vacation! I've got social security and medical coverage, like any good German!"

They say, in a chorus:

"When will you take off your imaginary nurse's uniform, and that stupid white cover on your head?"

"Tea?"

When we finish, both of us imagined a silky curtain falling. Before leaving, we asked her where she Works, and if we could see her again…

A Fat-Lady in red, dressed in red, will be standing by a thick tapestried door. She looks at a carpeted Escalator, there, below her feet in tight shoes. "You'll see other girls lounge around, dressed in hot red." The Fat –Lady in red, stands there, checking out the men, waiting, in a single file by the second door.

Music.

Loud American music.

She says: "Gut nacht!"

We nod.

"Take off our trousers."  East German underwear.

She unzips.

"Could she teach us English?" They say those Eastern European prostitutes speak English to American soldiers.

"With whom would you like me to begin?"

"Begin."

Both strip. Lie down.

One trembles a little.

The other smiles, as if he were already caressing her breasts.

Crumbling toilet paper.

Flushing.

She crouches.

Waits for one of us.

One kisses her.

The other

Caresses her back, his finger making its way down to her…

"I won!"

Milan wins over Madrid.

Yelling crowd.

One says to the other, "why hadn't they argued it out, in the street, in front of that giant mirror, to find Out who might be the first…"

"You cheated! I saw you sperming on the sheets!"

One says to the female, after a cup of coffee, "How long have you been in Berlin?"

"I win?"

"No. It's me!"

She turns on her back. She licks her red wet lips, now open for business.

Each one, on his side, prick in hand, angles.

Loud South Pacific.

(She says to herself: "we were all 16 years old, on our way to Berlin. They said we'd have nifty new Clothing, a fine apartment, with a new kitchen and windows overlooking trees in the courtyard. A dream For all of us, finally out of our blurred village, now thrown into the future. The bus driver, to be nice, got Us free rides on wooden horses. I so wanted to ride one through my village! Each one of use caught the Ring and we got another free ride, but Theresa found herself a rocking horse, rocked ahead of the Others, until she yelled

"This rocking horse is a winner!"

I asked: "How long in that bus?"

"Eat? Go to the toilets?"

The bus driver answered all our questions: "Fuck off!"

Got there.

We wore the same make-up.

The same clothing.

We sat on cushy red seats.

Everything looked like a theater set I dreamed of seeing.

"Don't ask what I was going to ask."

The others, already there, with black eyelashes, heavy red lipstick, and soft, clinging red

dresses, open at

The hips.

"Anything else?"

A huge, empty pool, with lots and lots of tables, in single file, all aligned on the floor.

"Did you ever hear me grunt? We weren't allowed."

"Did you ever say, in an Eastern European accent, "gratis pro Deo?"

I had a smattering of Latin in our tiny, village church. The priest wore black and wrote in tiny

letters, on The blackboard. My teacher always made us recite: "gratis pro Deo."

Later, I said: "Ich bin ein Istanbuler!"

In front of me, what looked like an East Berlin pool, at the crossing of Hindenburg and Luther.

"What about those tables?"

The Fat- Lady in red, how she would, at that very moment, let herself be carried away on the first steps Of the escalator! As if she was ready to dive in…

One of the other girls said: "They push the red button, and she allows them to choose a table." Tiny Lights on the ceiling.

The Fat-Lady in red, says: "The rich ones take the private elevator down to the table they wish to Occupy. There, they strip and wait. I welcome them. The Fat-Lady in red  asks them to pay me, right then And there!" She asks them: "what'll be? Which one?" She declares, in an East Berlin accent, the hourly Rates: 40 US dollars for half an hour.

I'm on my table, on my back. I keep my cunt open for inspection. I'm number 38.

"If one of my rich costumers wants more, we come to an agreement, in line with the prices the Fat- Lady In red had ALREADY defined.

To make moments more enticing, huge mirrors had been installed above each table.

I can see myself.

He can glimpse at himself, if he turns around.

She had clipped my index nail to ease my way in.

That's another price.

Sometimes, they like to keep their shirts on. Once in a while, their ties. Their ties tell me half the story,  Half a sentence.

Rolex, another.

She says to me, and to the others: "Don't forget to buy your toilet paper!"

Most probably, they're on a business trip. Don't forget their picture post-cards in their back pockets, gotten from another trip.

Monday afternoons, the rates go down.

"I forgot to tell you how we know what day it is! It's all in the music!!!"

Mondays: Mozart

Tuesday: Berlioz

Wednesday: Ravel

Thursday: Gershwin

Friday: Beethoven

Saturday: no music!

Chapter II

"This is mayor Mannheim, calling all editors listed below:

Bild

Zeit

New York Times

Paris edition of the Herald Trib.

Manchester Guardian

Le Monde

Atlanta Constitution

L'Humanité

Boston Herald

Hong-King Kong Daily

Moscow Free Press

Alaska Tea Press."

Table 28 calls for help, screams: "There's a fire on table 34. Call the fire department!"

At 4 AM, a Five Star Alarm.

"Call all local fire engines." (Some still asleep.)

Apparently, some elegant whore house had caught on fire because of too many cigars. In fact, on a cell Call from a businessman from Munich, socks still on, wearing an expensive Chanel tie. By chance, a red Ash, from his cigar, fell on his tie, setting it on fire.

Photographers were told, officially, to keep their distance.

Somebody screamed, from the depth of the pool.

(When Hitler got back from Munich, with what he believed was a dose of foresight, he ordered Honecker, and his workers to build him the largest pool in the West: 80 feet long, 12 foot lanes

(I had my Table in the 12th lane) and a magnificent 30 foot diving board. On October 6th, 1989, Honecker shook Hands with Gorbachev. His wife, Raisa, stood behind her husband and smiled.

The Fat-Lady in red whispered to herself: "I'll waste all my funds with that!"

Table 28 yells: "Why isn't that fucking fire department here?"

"The answer, my dear, is clearly written on my lips! Before leaving Berlin, the Russians, and, in Particular, an officer, decided to immortalize his remembrance of where he had fired on a residential Home. The decision was made. He ordered his soldiers. He ordered them to: "take up lots of stones From those houses. Make a 4ft mound, and spray it with any color you wish, as long as it'll keep any car, Any truck, immobile and nearly invisible. That'll slow down any car or truck from moving fast toward its Destination!" Fat-Lady in red called out to table 28: "Do not ask so many questions! They're on their Way!" However, four foot mounds, on the sidewalk, prohibited fire trucks from rapidly coming over.

A right tire blows out.

All the Eastern European young women, who were ready to please men with money, were asked either to crouch or lie on their backs, legs wide open, shaved. The Fat-Lady in red feared all those fire fighters might sperm the water, perhaps drowning her ladies on their tables, in their lanes.

She yelled out: "Open up all fire hoses."

Nearly all Eastern Europeans, 16 years old, drowned. Their tables floated away.

The girls were on their backs, like wilted flowers on a pond.

But my father had taught me how to swim.

I swam to the other side of the pool, where I knew there was a ladder. I climbed up. Threw myself on The elegant tiled ground and, still wet from all that sperm, breathed a huge sigh of relief. All the others, On their backs.

Dead.

They passed me by.

I saw, in my village's outdoor pool, dirt after each frequent rain.

I was the only survivor.

Afterwards, time on my hands, I decided to learn French and, in particular, 19th century French poetry. (Somebody told me Baudelaire was at the root of all modern English poetry.)

"Do you remember anything else?"

A husky carnival boss had his men unsaddle his half-painted wooden horses.

I was alone, walking down the sidewalk.

Other horses were amputated by the long trip.


Chapter III

A switch

ENTER

Quote: "A Musical Key."

SKINNY asks FATSO ask an impertinent question:" When was your first time?"

"The answer, my friend, is written in a dream of a foreign place, foreign farms, hobbled animals, poverty stricken people, walking back from non-existing fields."

"And you?"

"All I can remember, when my memory flags, is my freshman year in a university town. A fraternity accepted me, after much hazzzing! On Friday nights, lots of shnaps, dancing with local college girls, all Virgins, at least as of the first semester. I weighed 138 pounds, until 3 in the "morgen." All were happily disposed to climb up the stairs to a collective bedroom, one of three still available. At that time, if I remember correctly, I fucked until daylight. Then, boredom snuck in. Then, once again, I began putting On Weight."

A drizzle.

She whispered ten twelve lines from a Baudelaire sonnet.

A trans-Turkish translation?

An adolescent dream: she quoted Proust's definition of an artistic relation: "A law joining different Facts."

She repeated my memory: "a reality, a relation, a law joining different facts."

She closed her eyes. She laughed in her own language.

"Just a bunch of meaningless lines, that's all."

She said to herself.

How would she earn enough to get out of this world?

At times, she thought she might provide a Table of Contents, perhaps even a bibliography. But having Read "Madame Bovary," she dreamt of becoming someone else. Maybe, as she mulled prose over a Thought, a publisher might publish her diary? Her book might attract the eye of a film executive, and she would be invited to Venice, Paris or Toronto, when the film came out for some or other award.

She believed, at times, in the bathtub, she'd become a movie star, recognized in Istanbul, as she walked down a street, in red transparent high heel shoes.

The Fat-Lady in red, who had survived, stood at attention, at the top of her circular staircase, looking Out, as a captain would, at his crew, down below.

Had she ever dreamt that dream?

At times, in the early hours of a dreamy morning, she remembered excited voices at the edge of her Village.

She saw hairy men pitch tents on her parade ground.

Circus music.

Chickens.

A week later, they folded their tents, threw out what remained of hot dogs, sauerkraut, buns.

Dogs crunched up all the rest.

(Perhaps, a wished-for scenario?)

She learned a new French word from an elderly man, breathing heavily on top of her. Was he going to Die of an acute prostate cancer, or just an overly-curved penis? He said he knew Paris by heart.

He suggested I should rent a room near Montmartre. An upstairs room with a tiny window, overlooking The Sacré Coeur. The landlady told us, all of us, in those same tiny rooms, the shower and the toilets were at the end of the corridor. To be shared.

As you entered the room, somebody had left behind a huge poster of Josephine Baker in a Banana Outfit.

In my mind's eye, I saw powerful lights on a stage, and a lady dressed in banana skins.

I said to myself, for no apparent reason, that poster was probably a screened memory. Could it be mine?

Then, in advance, she asked for a month's rent.

I said, in a voice I could barely recognize as my own, would she take Turkish money or, perhaps, Turkish Express?

The landlady smelled of cabbage soup.

Her hand stretched out.

I gave her the few euros I still had in my bag.

For some inexplicable reason, I dreamt of a Turkish prostitute, walking down side streets in Montmartre, not far from those second-rate portrait painters, on the square.

I learned at my university, where I had seriously begun my studies, that language was ambiguous and, For example, my professor told the class that the Place de la Concorde, during the French Revolution, was the site of death. What a way to translate "Concorde!" The king's head, on a spike, paraded by fancy stores-to-be.

I checked out my notes in my spare time.

A woman, with a rucksack, slowly walked by a bar, with a huge mirror behind the bartender, one elbow on the counter.

In the mirror, I saw myself wearing a fancy dress.

Red high heel shoes.

An alligator handbag, with a gold key chain, swaying on its side.

(Could I ever have any idea of what I was to become, at least for the time being?)

Not that long after ("after" what?) that, the elderly grey-haired Chair of the French department, with enough influence, hired me. I was assigned to an office which I shared with two other language instructors. We shared a phone. The possibility of sharing the Xerox machine for distributing a Baudelaire sonnet in class. I was also given an old computer, salvaged from a US university gift. A hook for my tattered Turkish hand-woven coat.

When I passed by my colleagues, in the corridors, I felt as if they saw right through me. Some of my colleagues undressed me, with eyes filled with desire.

At best, I felt as if I were an extra, with a walk-on part, and no voice.

There, I saw myself dressed for the occasion, a skimpy red outfit, shadowed nipples, and

wearing black panties, bought in a local mall.

I attacked an elderly lady, dressed in red. Her husband had run away with one of the girls, lying down on her back in our waterless pool.

I remembered myself, with a highly wealthy customer who had refused to take off his socks. He kept his tie on.

Next, I powdered my nose, looked at myself in a store window. There, I saw myself standing next to three half-naked mannequins, waiting to be dressed, in the latest fashion.

Sometimes, I really thought I was actually walking down a Parisian street, or a university corridor! Nobody talked to me, not even raising an eyebrow, when I passed by. A Humanities professor in the Latin and Greek department, with a specialty in Church history from the 10th to the 12th century,

saw me walking. He looked the other way, as if…as if…I were the Black Plague, under some French author's pen.

I heard a Mozart concerto.

I listened.

Then I heard the phone ring.

It happened, regularly, around 6 in the morning, before I got up to brush my hair and teeth, especially after a cavity.

"Turn off that fuckin' Mozart! I'm trying to sleep!"

I spit out my mouthwash.

A friend, in my village, had given me, as a birthday gift, a yellow Johnson and Johnson dental floss.

At least, at that early hour, I knew I had a mouthful of teeth!

Last night, I smelled my favorite Turkish dish: eggplants, stuffed with rice, on top of pieces of lamb.

My appetite told me I was alive!

All I had to do was to stare in my pocket mirror, and mull over Sade's "La Nouvelle Justine." I, too,

glanced at myself, in a huge mirror, covering the wall.

 Or, in a dream, I was I visiting a Park Avenue psychiatrist, with a thick East German accent. On the street level on 86th street and…so expensive! (I whispered to myself, was he building a summer residence in East Hampton?)

Outside, I dreamt of Turkish names. Maybe, some had been my classmates?

Inside, he spoke with energy: "Pleaze siz down! Vaz its your name? Spel it. "

"Tel me vatz di mater."

He waved me to a leather couch.

I answered: "I don't feel myself!"

How I would have loved to speak my own language!

"Iz gut beghining!"

"Plez liv di moni by di dour."

Whose tongue?

My next visit was scheduled for 6:30, the following morning.

I said to myself, he puts in lots of hours. Puts all that money in the bank.

Then, he told me he never had time to go on vacation: "peepl needz me!"

As he talked, I knew he was  imagining his bank account. Years of asking the same questions, anything to hear, not even about one of Wilhelm Reich` orgasm.

He knew we hid behind ourselves.

He said: "He knows you hide behind yourself."

Would I ever get to that mirror stage? Actually, I did do it- taking a cold shower, that late steamy morning.

Steam…

With my index, I drew my face on the steamed mirror.

I smelled coffee, working its way up the stairs.

The concierge hadn't yet taken out the garbage. That "fragrance" snucked up to my floor!

Then, I heard it flush down the mouth of the incinerator.

No problem for her! Business as usual! No need for a psychologist!

My shrink!

Somebody said that that reminded him of an ancestral practice, probably in Australia, where heads were shrunk!  How many articles from the pen of tenured anthropologists!

Or, was the whole thing a reminder of an old movie I had never seen?

Then, maybe, I saw my head shrunk to another size. I saw a bearded lady, dressed in red, standing next to a midget, swallowing fire! Customers paid, and hoped they would be shrunk into another identity!

A regular simulacrum.

I was 16 years old.

I said I wanted to study in Paris, to find out all about French theories!

Besides, I loved pommes frites!

I asked myself, would I ever know what images I was trying to express in another language  A technical one… I read those Russian theorists, those Danes, those Germans… I CAME TO REALIZE ONE ANALYTICAL VOCABULARY WIPED OUT ANOTHER!

They said all of that, seated on high stools in McDonald's, facing the Sorbonne.

Freud, Marx, Saussure, Barthes, Lacan…

Was the "Purloined Letter" actually purloined? Or was it somewhere in my loins?

They said my childhood hadn't really belonged to me, that I had been genomed…

I quoted Wordsworth from my damaged memory: "The world is too much with us late and soon…"

Or an image, a disturbing one, from a Grimm fairy tale.

I invented my memory.

Dreams switched them around, threads of my past, unraveled.

"Doctor," as I called him, I said I was Little Red Riding Hood, eaten by a wolf in dream clothing.

To escape, I talked about drugs in my 9 o'clock class.

I asked, if we believe in God, would He be responsible for all the horrors in the world?

Were there any providential roads, leading to an answer, beginning with the plague or the death of a baby?

Were we all framed, with no way out of a Biblical cord or, like Ham, framed, after seeing his father naked and drunk?

A student raised her hand from the back of the class: "If that's true, why did Samuel Rosentock,  fom Moiesti, in Eastern Romania, change his name to Tristan Tzara? or Ducasse into comte de Lautréamont?"

She asked whether all those name changes had something to do with a rejection of the Father?

Did, I too, wish to reject my past, and think of myself as an "Other Myself?"

Another question: is there "rire" in "décrire"?

The class laughed in unison.

At that very moment, the door swung open, and Herr Shmaltz, a distinguished Professor of 20th century theater, walked in.

Scarf, doubled around his neck, like French students do. There he was, motionless and silent, and then he said,

"I was passing by, when I heard your class erupt in laughter. You all sounded like a peasant chorus from  a carnival scene in a Bruegel painting!"

And then he added:" That is strictly forbidden in this august university."

And he added: "Teaching is no laughing matter."

He pointed to me and, in front of the whole class, told me to come to his office, as soon as my noisy class was over.

A future seduction manquée?

In "Hoch Deutsch," he asked me, in his elegant office, with a worn-out leather couch, three elegant  holstered chairs, a whimsical tapestry on the wall, and behind his desk, a life- size portrait of Friedrich

Schiller- and a quote from his favorite play: "Die Rauber."

I asked: "Was folgt weiter"?

"Remember, as part of the past of your mind, do not repeat: "Und lass es auch  Prostitution heissen."

Then he said: "Please, sit down."

"Where?"

"There." (He pointed to an uncomfortable leather chair.)

Then, I asked: "Where's the "There?" there?

He talked, and I made believe I heard him.

(Was he talking to me or to another Me?)

" Please, tell me about your "me?"

He shied away from the direction of my female gaze.

"Do you have a boyfriend?"

Somewhere, I thought to myself: "who the fuck does he think I am?"

Actually, my girlfriend and I met at the Indiscrete Bijou. Ever since, that's where we'd meet! I'm going there, now.

(Was I thinking of a Diderot novel?)

The Chair said: "I'll repeat what she said, as if, somehow, there were two voices in her. Had she inherited a form of controlled madness? Or was it simply madness under control, perhaps?"

I'm sure that one of the students will ask me to get a lawyer, to get away from an accusation of sexual harassment.

What would happen, were there to be an article in the Bild?

I can imagine hearing whispers in the corridor. My colleagues…

Would there be a full page ad, out of someone's jealousy? A promotion side-tracked.

After that professional indiscretion, would there be others? How many other indiscretions in front of Schiller?

He whispers to himself- when I finish my administrative duties, Friday afternoons, I go home, take a shower, soap myself, as if,

What I was thinking,

What I actually did in my office, might go away. I dreamt.

Then I'd go swimming in Fat-Lady in red's dried-out pool.

("Fritzel, don't you hear the two rings at the servants' door? It's the deli man. Go!"

Two minutes later, Red ate, with relish, a wiener schnitzel and a vanilla ice dream topped by a mountain of whipped cream. Then she wiped her chin and smiled.)

That pool, unless I'm mistaken, was the jewel of Honecker's East Berlin, built by Hitler himself?

Next to that gym, there was a fortress-like high security prison for homosexuals, gypsies, and Jews.

Diminuitive Mme Fat- Lady in red or, as we called her, Mme Sex, yelled out to Fritzel: "Didn't you hear…" the She introduced me to a young Turk.

Ever since, I'm there, every Friday night.

 On my back.

"How much?"

"Depends on what I ask her to do! If she's on her knees, that's an extra $ 20.00.  Slip it into a red-Covered box, nailed to my table.

"More"?

"The same sum."

"I don't like her to talk."

"Sometimes, it's inevitable, I mean, when I remove my underwear …?

"What does she say?"

She says, in broken Nazi- German, she feels like a "thing" disconnected. Her voice fades away. She Remembers

That night when a traveling circus came to her village.

Loud music.

"Anything about her family?"

"Not a word."

But she did say that, when she got to Berlin, famished, and poorly dressed, she saw as many movies as She could! She got to love Harrison Ford and Betty Grable.

Shops were fabulous!

Restaurants!

Bars!

Especially the one she had spotted, with a gigantic mirror behind the counter.

She asked me, if we could see all the sites in Berlin. And a night club…

"Let's take a trolley."

"What does your wife think about your activities?"

"She died a month ago in a car crash, on the autobahn, outside Munich."

Then, she shut up and wanted to go back in time, when she had lived another life.

I said: "I had hitched a ride, or so I thought but, right there, a young Swede, with a huge sign saying:                                    "Nach Paris."

I said:" What a beautiful handwriting!"

He said: "My father always admired my script!"

The other day, when I turned 17, he said it was time for me to become a man. He said that, in a few years, I'd be taking over our factories.

I lit a cigarette. I said: "Father's money! Not as rich as Alfred Nobel, but my father has three factories making matches."

I replied: "A man's a man, and all that!"

He gave me an address in Paris. "They'll do a proper job!"

 A, 1937 white Mercedes convertible stopped.

"Hop in!"

"May I ask you, where are you going?"

Then he said he'd run out of gas, and if were willing to pay for it at the next gas station?

We did.

He smiled.

Gas tank to the brim.

Then he drove away, leaving us  behind.

ENTER

QUOTE: Joyce Mansour: "The first poet pissed on his love." Or Lacan's: "The significance of the phallus."

We came up with the cash.

We paid for his gas.

How lucky we were!

A truck stopped, and drove us to Strasbourg.

I said to that 17 year old Swede, I'd repay him the minute we got to Paris. What I hadn't realized, it would be July 14, and everything would be closed!

But I had no money!

"You can pay me tomorrow!"

He gave me an address.

"Without a doubt."

Next day, we hitched a ride into France.

Next day, it turned out to be July 14th.

I said to myself: "I'll *repay him the minute I get to Paris.*"

*He gave me his address.*

*Next day, I went to a place somebody had suggested I go.*

It turned out to be a whore house!

"Men only!"

With a pool in the front yard.

Now, I'm back at the Indiscrete Bijou.

The Chair says: "I'd like you to meet my daughter!"

He said: "He'd paid a French woman to carry his baby, for a reasonable sum."

He said: "Here's my daughter, Lena!"

We organize birthday parties. Last year,

I gave her the latest Pear computer, two French dresses, a tee shirt, with a picture of  Lou Reed, and Three books on the history of France.

When there's a teacher's meeting, I'd go. I heard she's an excellent student.

"Lena?"

'That's her name. She knows how to make a ratatouille with virgin Greek olive oil!"

When there's a periodic conference with her teacher, she says she's an excellent student.

"My own Lena, we also call her "Helena, after my aunt!"

I said: "You've just painted the portrait of my own, Lena!" (I adopted her from a sick mother.)

"They are --yours and mine-- mirror images of each other!"

He says: "I've got an idea, and I hope your daughter will join mine, and all of us will go to Paris! My wife Left me a bundle and, after her death, the two of us got parts of it. The other parts were given to a Homeless shelter, and needy Romans. I bought a modest flat on rue Vaugirad, facing the Luxembourg Gardens. Both could go riding on donkeys in the park, and eat ice-creams, sitting on rusty chairs!  The Two girls could sit down and watch  puppets hitting each other, a traditional Italian tradition! They can Eat all the frites they wanted, and there's a small stand, facing Notre Dame, where we can eat hot dogs with Dijon mustard!"

Now Paris.

Now, on rue Vaugirad.

Now, looking at the Luxembourg gardens, through French windows.

I looked out the window. I didn't see a single motorized chair. I had seen them in Istanbul, and none on Madison Avenue. I saw walkers on Broadway, and not a single one on Park Avenue. I saw canes on West End Ave. Three on Avenue…"

Now, looking at kids, each one riding a pony.

Now, asking the two girls to quit their shouting.

THEN…        ENTER A

QUOTE: "Imitate life!"

Three days later, the chair asked me if I was willing to marry him.

I murmured." You're kindly mad!"

He insisted.

"I first looked at you, getting off the trolley, wearing tight black American gym pants."

He added:

"Your body was an erotic anecdote!"

(He mulled: "No middle-aged man could resist! Better than a center fold in a porn magazine!")

"Then, I walked by your class. You were seated on the edge of a table, legs crossed.  Male students must Have gone bananas!"

"Crazy, staring at your… Behind a black board with a hand-written Baudelaire sonnet."

She mused, for an instant, and then erupted in laughter: "You must be…!"

"There's more!"

"I once saw you getting off the trolley."

 "I heard you talking to a woman, you said: "What do you think of Roland Barthes's theory of the 'reality Effect'?  And I overheard your excited conversation about Derrida's Marx…"

(I whispered to myself, what a fabulous pseudo-intellectual!)

I suspected you were late for class!

(Actually, I thought to myself, I must be another "I.")

In the faculty dining room, you ate alone, your tray…

Actually, I thought to myself, I, too, may be another!

"How's that for a hypothesis?"

"That's a way of clearing out one's emotions!"

"Did I ever talk to you about my family, I mean, seriously, about my father, my mother, my two sisters, a Brother, and my aunt, who lived with us, when her husband died during the war? The last war…"

He whispered: "Fate seems so simple, too matter of fact! Can any language speak to another?"

"Well, about myself, first! I was a feared critic of all those cultural historians who swiped footnotes from

An "elsewhere!" The ones on the international talking circuit, conferences, intimate meetings, deciding Next year's program, the 10 titles on the menu, to be printed and placed on each of the round tables, in The Mayflower Hotel, in Washington.  We interviewed the candidates we had previously chosen, based on their letters of recommendations and their academic work.

Or, at another annual meeting, sponsored by the…I will not divulge the names of all those autobiographical novelists who were honored, inducted into an appropriate society, holding its annual Convention in D.C. The "Poet of America" was also selected, even though the decision was often a matter of age, geography, sex, skin color and religion.

I heard someone brag that her first 800 pages, of an uninteresting novel, might be turned into a movie! (Most likely, a yesterday's graduate from a New York State college, specializing in creative "writing.")

I heard you sing the "Song of Roland."

Then, the "Chanson de Roland!" all in the original, next to Bédier's French translation.

You made the class weep over photos of the Spanish Civil War.

You made them see and write about a Picasso painting of a Spanish bombed-out-village, now in a Spanish museum.

A student raised her hand.

"Can I tell you a true story?"  She said.

(I suspected she had already written a first draft.)

"My grandfather, who came from Turkey, was captured by Nazis in Paris, and sent to Drancy, waiting to Be exterminated."

I began reading WWII writings.

Nadia, one of my girlfriends, came back from Hell.

She had been pregnant.

A single shot in her belly.

The good people of Armenia, machine-gunned in their town square.

After the war, women who had collaborated with the Nazis (or, were they simply, German soldiers?) had their hair shaved off, and paraded through the streets of their towns.

In Paris, parents went to the Hotel Lutetia to read names and faces, to see if they could identify those who may have returned from the camps.

(At times, when I misplace my keys, like an old woman, searching deep into her bag until…

Oui! I found them.)

Now, in the apartment.

ENTER

QUOTE:  Charles Olson's "The Maximus Poems."  (Pick the one you like the most!)

Now, looking through French windows, curtains parted.

Now, asking the girls to keep their voices down.

Three days later, he turned to her and, with insistence, and a sense of anxiety (you can tell by the hesitations in his voice) asked her if she would marry him.

"Are you…" (She tried to find the right word in German.)

He nodded and said, ceremoniously, "I mean it!"

I first saw you getting off the trolley, wearing one of those revealing black American-style gym tights. You were an unsuspecting erotic invitation, and no middle-age could resist playing with that mellifluous Vision! Then, on a more professional side, I caught a glimpse of your class, whispering "Lacan's Sade!"  The other day, I saw you arrive at the university. You were late for your class. Running! No gym suit at that moment! I also saw you eating alone in the faculty dining room. For a moment, I thought you were Somebody else! After all, I thought to myself, you really might have been someone else! After all is said and done, all of us may seem double to our friends! How's that for an academic hypothesis!!"

"No! I'm like the like you see before you."

"Did I ever talk to you about my father, my mother, my two sisters, my brother? Retrospectively, fate seems to be slow in getting to that narrative point!"

"I heard you singing the "Song of Roland," to make a point!"

"Could one of yours have been captured and sent to a Polish extermination camp?"

"Perhaps."

"Because of the lack of information that I possess, I sometime ask myself why wasn't I there, with Them?"

("In a documentary, I saw smoke rising from Polish industries of death.")

"You would have gotten perfectly on, with my father, now that I know how you appreciate decadent Art In Berlin, in the twenties! His love of going every Friday night to the Black café, when he got to Berlin! Dad also, behind our backs, collected erotic works of art, some, as far away, from Japan! He said it was a Regular activity in pre-war Berlin!

In a secret cellar vault, he kept works by Max Beckmann and Otto Dix: people fucking asses, as he used to say in his loud dreams!

"Charming and lucid revelations!"

 "What are you working on, now?"

"I'm reading, and I hope, for the last time, Rousseau's  sexy "Confessions.""

"And, to keep me abreast of contemporary passions in the US, I' m reading a book on

Satan everywhere!!! In fact, I've even plundered the Koran and proposed  a sixth sura."

"Why six?"

"Why not?"

Besides, I like three plus three or 2 multiplied by three."

ENTER

QUOTE:"A madrigal is a secular vocal…"

She says: "Did you know you snore?"

She undressed, about to go to bed next to him.

He swears he'll never snore again!

He's got a prominent, flabby paunch, and waltzing baggy balls! Washes his teeth, otherwise… he stinks From the mouth!

Quotes Schiller.

He then hums Bethoven's "Heroica."

Somebody blows himself up.

Only Eldad escapes for a cup of Turkish coffee.

"Anyone else escaped?"

"Kaphira and then Aruns. They should be the first ones to know! They're distant cousins! One grew a Cistersian beard, and looked like Freud. The other one spoke in British popular.

He had thick sideburns and took himself for M. Mi-Cawber. Mother was fond of both! She's still alive. Should I give her the bad news?"

"Do it!"

"I'll do it,

after six."

Time has another dimension for her! She's finishing reading Schoenberg's "Journal," and she's looking Forward to savoring his play, "Der biblische Weg." It's all about the Jewish State, something she had always suspected, having read Herzel.

"Did she ever come across Gershom Sholem's work on the Kabbalah?"

She lit a Gauloise.

"You'll never believe this, but she smoked it, after having read Schoenberg's play, and then, she'd attack Heidegger's "Identity and Difference."

As you may have guessed it, the whole family was infatuated with the question of identity!

Who's who?

Who's a "who"? whom do you think is another "who"?

But, then again, my father and mother were fabulous skiers in the Dolomites. Night and day.

"Can I change the subject, and tell you what's equally important for me?"

"Go ahead!"

"Berlin! Somebody told me all about Berlin…Everything he told me about all those Turks in Berlin was a partial lie. Somebody else insisted, everything about Berlin was a true museum! I guess you'd never know me, when I first arrived in Berlin and…walked down those streets, before learning French Literature.

I lived in a "chambre de bonne."

"You said, or someone else said: When I begin living in Berlin, I'd be born again!

"Then I'd swim."

Then we took a train.

I accompanied you to the Kaiser Hotel's main dining room, with 38 tables and little signs, sitting on top of them, indicating what university we came from! You had already told me you were going to interview the finalists, for a non-tenured position in the French department, someone who had recently gotten a Ph.D in the invention of "Love in the Middle Ages."

I sat next to you.

Another candidate,

Chosen among 200 applicants, was being interviewed. He would teach the literary

revolutionary Tradition in 19th century French literature. She was offered a tenured position,

which had to be Acceptable, by lunch, by the committee.

All that, I had hoped, would be my April in Paris! But it might as well have been a fiction in

Berlin!

ENTER

QUOTE:"Forgive me, too!"

FATSO: "If only…"

SKINNY: "I disagree."

(Here, I remembered my mirror image in a bar. Now, the mirror had been scotch-taped…Was

this my Berlin?

The bar barred.

A sign in the window:

"Closed."

 Was that in my Berlin dream?

A child's dream of glories, and a beautiful apartment, overlooking trees in the courtyard?

Could I ever walk back there? Only the perfume of that beer lingered on. Even my drunken

father passed by that Circus.

(It reminded him of the dream he had had growing up, and without a penny to his name.

Now, he hobbled back from the village market, singing. He would have loved to be reborn elsewhere, with another name, another geography.)

"Did I ever tell you another of my experiences, before you hired me? I told you before, in Berlin, I was particularly sensitive to puddles! Well, lo and behold! Here I was, walking down a sidewalk in Berlin, when a jeep, with a US army captain (I later found that out) splashed me, as he drove through a big puddle, soaking me from head to feet! He stopped. Got out. Excused himself, and asked if I didn't want to follow him to his place, where he could clothe me again! I thought I was crazy to accept! Up a flight of steps. Key in hand. We walked into his apartment. He took out of his closet an Army shirt, jogging pants. Offered me a cup of tea. Or did I prefer army rationed coffee? I said:" No sugar, please!"

 Frank Sinatra sang.

We talked a lot.

He took a picture of me, and I said : "I have my father's Leica."  (Had he only waited for a NY Times, October17, 1I3th, section B11, where the Lieca Panasonic Lumix DMC-LF1 sold for $500.00 !) " Maybe," he said, we could walk around Berlin and take pictures. Old and new, like before, after, and now."

("Listen, FATSO, do it for my sake! I gave up --on you know what-- and decided to enroll in a Columbia College course in fencing. I got a scholarship from a rich Chinese who had paid for one of those high rises in Manhattanville. I get there. Somebody takes me by the arm and says: "You're it! Every Saturday, during the Fall Season, you'll be selling hot dogs, with mustard and sourkraut, together with Columbia banners. Check out the stands! Afterwards, we try to give everyone working, a free hot dog!"

"What the hell are you talking about? You're a stinking foreigner! Who the hell ever wrote you a letter of recomendation ? You're a German. How's your American? Besides, some Admissions officer would check out your credentials! Does your American allow you to live where you want to? In some frat. house, on 113 street, off Broadway, where fraternities live and fuck in upstairs brownstones?"

FATSO: "Listen, SKINNY, I've got it all worked out! Somebody, in the German dept, wrote your application! Somebody else filled out your request for financial aid! Then, you must have waited to the end of March or the beginning of April, for an answer. I read the official letter. You were told to try again, next year and, in the meantime, brush up on your Shakespeare! Those were his very words!"

By the time we got to Berlin, in that smelly bus, I couldn't believe it! Here I was, so far from my village! I never thought I'd be a born-again Turk!

"Between you and me, did I ever tell you what the bus driver mumbled, during the whole ride?

He listed his favorite painters! Can you believe that?"

Kirchner

Heckel

Beckmann

Feininger

Egon Schiele (at room temperature, in the cellar.)

I remembered, while he named his favorites, what Nietzsche had said: " if we wanted to move ahead, repeat what Freud was going to write, a while later: "forgetting is something half- way between history and memory where, to forget was never a victory."  I went a bit further, and said to myself, to forget was a loss of reality. I said to myself, where's then,the truth?

"Talking about truth, did I ever tell you what my father did during the war?  First, his parents volunteered him to fight on the Russian front. He'd be like Napoleon! He was born in 1928. When he got there, there weren't enough ambulances to take back our troops, not even dead ones!  They were, like Napoleon's troops, covered with snow, and many of them without shoes."

 In Berlin, I saw what remained of bombed-out buildings, and mounds of bricks, piled up to make cars and trucks slow down.

"Did I ever tell you what it was like, after the war? First, millions of tons dropped from the skies. Everywhere, windows blown out, floors caved in. On sidewalks, piles of rubble. You could see people looking for what they hoped they might find in the street. Only songs remained. Was it a reminder of a Brecht socialist musical? Then, what remained of sex shops, midnight performances, in dark night clubs. A very old lady dreamt about a chocolate bar she had left on the kitchen table.

"Let me interrupt."

"In your own cellar, apart from your father's Leica, did you find anything else?"

She answered:" My doll's carriage. Her Armenian wedding dress. My mother's favorite pot!"

"Was that all?"

"In that stinking bombed-out cellar, I smelled my dead dog."

"Anything else?"

"My father's prized edition of Lessing's works."

"Any other books?"

" My father had only finished high school, but he loved poetry! Around the table, on Sunday dinners, he'd recite Rilke's letter to his father and also his "Neue Gedichte." And, for his imagined readers, he'd give them "When Lilacs Last in the Dooryard Bloom'd."

"And you?"

"Actually, in comparison, I really had no life before West Point made me an officer. But I do remember my father, every Sunday, lighting his fat cigar and sitting in the TV room, munching on pop corn, watching a football game."

"As for me, I drove, with my girlfriend to see an outdoor movie and, make out!"

As they said somewhere: "That's All Folks!"

As for me, when the sky darkened, my memory returned. Somebody had planted a wooden plank over what remained of my bombed-out- cellar.

(When the sky darkened, memory crept back. A wooden plank over rubble. Cellars blown out. We searched for our belongings: a kid's elephant. Baby clothing. Somebody spotted a pot with burned-out potatoes. What had happed to my next door neighbor, Mr. Golz? Had he been taken away? My hands were shaking. Artillery had been set-up up in the street."

At that moment, I puked.

The Russians pillage our neighborhood.

They took all our white linen sheets to clean their rifles.

They yelled: "Hitler's dead!"

As I spoke, the sky darkened, rumbled, threatening our memories of the recent past: the present. Then, all went black. Birds on a branch, like a haiku, tweeted. Would we have been caught, at a moment, when history would begin all over again? Or Creation? Thunderous claps. Every leaf, every branch fell. People crouched in their doorways. I remember bombs by the Red Army Faction. Christian Klar and Brigitte Mohnhoupt, or simply a Berlin rebirthed!

Words pollute words.

Somebody, next to me, suspected God was in his punishing mood, after the 6th day…

All that, was left to my imagination, soon to become memory.

"Yes. I was table 32 or was it 38?"

She clutched her leather-bound Lutheran Bible.


Chapter V

What seemed to me to be a very brief moment, I was asked to state my name, where I lived, my phone number.

 I could hear a dimmed-out German song.

 I answered: "Leica, Kunt Strasse. 42, 4th floor. 06/22/89/72.

"Why Leica?" I was asked.

"Father's"

"Do you still have that camera?"

FATSO: "how much do you think she charges?  Does she have a pimp? Do you think she lives far-away? A double bed?  Stilleto heels? "

SKINNY: "I can imagine her getting on and off a trolley, wearing a Bangladeshy SCARF! They see themselves, in a broken mirror, and all's that left of a good bar."

FATSO: "I remember, from a magazine I flipped through, as I was having my hair cut: a French painting."

They closed their mouths.

"You'll never believe this, but for my 7th birthday, my grandfather gave me a Baby Browny, made by Kodak in Rochester."

"I hear

A possessed

Scream:

"Cyclorama

Diorama

Myrionama

Panorama

And, for a finale:

Eidophuskon."

"What was it like to go around the streets in Berlin after the war?"

I remember my grandfather smiling, when he spoke about how he shot as many Armenians as he could, with that rifle, hanging there, above the fireplace.

But grandfather remembered, upside down. His memory distorted his memories and thus, all of us, knowing that, everything he said we had to reverse. Armenia was, in truth, Turkey.

(Both imagined her on her knees.)

She says: "When I was 16, I rode my bike to the souk. I checked out all the rugs. I drank apple tea. 60 lanes. 4000 shops."

ENTER

QUOTE: "Amico, hai vinto; io ti perdon, perdonna…"  ("Friend, you have won: I forgive you, forgive me, too.")

(FATSO turns to SKINNY: "You've got a dirty MIND! Remember that sex shop? Why didn't you…"

SKINNY says: "I didn't know if they would put in three magazines in a large black envelope!")

He once remembered that a member of his family had immigrated to Manhattan. He lived on the top floor. He ate figs for breakfast. He discovered other Turks who owned grocery stores. Once a month, they'd write back to their families. Our neighbors read those letters, outloud. Through those letters, we lived through those letters—Manhattan, skyscrapers, drugs on the Lower East Side, near Tompkins Square. And Jewish tailors on Orchard Street, not far from a Turkish restaurant, with great borscht!"

FATSO says: "You've got a filthy imagination! Besides, I hear someone humming a Broadway hit."

She says:" The day after it rained, I had a big a puddle, right in front of our door! Besides, all that biking killed my ass!"

In fact, as the family said, in Manhattan, he really lived in a cockroach apartment with rats scampering all around him.

Only one light in the kitchen, the only place he could read and, sometimes, letters from back home.

In the street, he saw amputated dogs.

He wrote that he had gotten married to a blonde, who came from a farm in Poland, not way away from Warsaw. He said, in his one room apartment, there was a shower at the end of the corridor. Both showered together. Both dried themselves with a large yellowed towel.

When it rained, we recited a German poem we all knew by heart:

"Es regnet

Es regnet

Alles uber die Welt."

At night, when I got up from table 38, and took off my swim suit, I'd give Turkish lessons to a Hamburg businessman who was planning to open up a chain of food stores in Ankara.

("Listen, SKINNY! You'll never guess what I saw at the crossing of Marx and Hegel! An American captain, photographing something I couldn't imagine. He had a little brown camera! His girlfriend carried a long, silent, extended lens. What she was shooting at, I'll never know. All I could see was a street where there were broken signs of bombed-out buildings.")

SKINNY: "Listen! Your eyes need glasses! I know Marx read Hegel, and borrowed lots from him, otherwise there wouldn't have been a Marxist theory."

"You said 2."

I recited the only other one:

"Da Steig ein Baum. O reine, Unbersteigung!"

She prefered "Es."

By then, the sun had dried out all puddles, wherever they were.

(The nurse tells him to take off his pants and his shorts, to make sure he hadn't been injured anywhere else.)

She was dressed, like a prostitute, lying there, on her back.

She looked like a refugee from the East.

(Both of us took the worn-out porcelain handles of the bathtub and poured water, in another tub, used for washing laundry in Berlin.)

(The next day, they read about a bar where a huge mirror had been shattered. Shards, like somebody's rotten German!)

At night, it was a totally different story.

She said she shoved her father, spoke to him in a humming voice.

Still, he continued spinning out his dream.

(Rotten odors out of his mouth.)

She lullabied him.

Interrupted his dream, when he began yelling dates, places. He narrated, as if he were being interviewed in front of the main doors of City Hall. He wakes up his dream, and says to the interviewer: "Here, right here, I was given my uniform, gloves, a fancy hat and a new rifle. I was instructed on how to kill,  then clean my rifle. Let me recite the names of all the places."

"What about syphilis?"

They dreamt about a hero, walking on hot coals, to prove to a husband that he hadn't raped his wife in the forest. They did remember she had dyed her hair blond.

The Armenians were our goal.

(As she walked, she murmured lyrics she had memorized from an Ella Fitzgerald record.)

The mud was boot-high in Armenia. They say it was a massacre.

He threw his blanket on the floor.

Pulled the sheet over his head.

He nearly chocked me.

He kept sliding off the bed.

He kicked me.

Sometimes, I yelled at my father.

He snored with pleasure, as if he hadn't the slightest idea of who he was.

I leaned over, and put the blanket back on his body.

He sobbed.

More screams.

HE SOBBED.  HE LAUGHED.

He whispered: "Hurrah for the Turkification of our enemy!"

I stared at my eyes in a broken mirror.

Father always came back, smelling of raki.

Mother said we needed money. He had spent it all in the village bar where the men, wearing clogs, danced, talked, and sang childhood songs.

"Don't start that again!" She'd say.

"Come home, when the market closes."

Mother said:" If he wanted to eat a bowl of soup, she'd warm up the barley, and give him a slice of black bread."

"No," he said.

"I'm going to sleep," he said.

"Don't forget, when I was a young man, I studied geography."

His mind wandered.

He stopped remembering.

After dinner, he smoked a home-rubbed cigar and farted. His forehead fell on the kitchen table.

Mother washed the soup bowl.

In Berlin, when I get out of bed, I often wondered if my father and mother had ever really loved each other.

My older brother was the only one they ever cared for.

"I think I told you how I got to Berlin in a beaten- up bus."

The night was lit up with star candles.

FATSO: "Too many words spoil the brew."

SKINNY:"They rained down on everybody!  Is there a reason? Maybe a simple answer: that's human nature.")

When I got to Berlin, and walked around to get my bearings, I thought I'd wind up in a police file.

My father got a postcard, telling him to go to City Hall, that Saturday, to get a medal pinned on his left lapel.

I only knew it rained like hell that morning, and I decided not to jump over all those puddles. My mother did it, and had to put her clogs near the fire, to dry them out.

Then a rainbow.

I never gave them my address. I remembered seeing myself in a huge mirror, wondering if that was really me, or some sort of an imitation! Or a Police station?

For a long time, I stayed in the shadows.

When I thought nobody could hear me, I sang a Turkish song.

ENTER

QUOTE: "I've nothing to add."

Suddenly, a man, with a long broom, working the sidewalks, heard me singing, and began singing with me.

We walked our own language.

He lived with other Turks, in a tiny room.

He said:" Neo-Nazis had burned down another house, where so many of us stayed, until early morning, when we all had a piece of bread, and a cup of three-day old coffee, before going to work."

He said "I should meet Ayten Köse."

I knew that, with a little money, I could bus myself back to Istanbul.

"We're treated like whores in Berlin, even when I finally got properly dressed.

Hear them smiling at us and yelling: "You fuckin' whores."

Then, I stopped singing, and he went on brooming sidewalks.

That afternoon, nearly all the puddles had dried up.

A group of youngish boys, who had escaped Hitler's jugend, were throwing stones and broken pieces of windows, found in the street.

"Hey you, cunt of a female! This aint no place to take pictures with your Leica! And you, with that premature brown baby, that goes for you, too."

I just wanted to have my guest-of-honor walk down this street of many souvenirs! One day, perhaps, it will recall its name! And then, we can walk to museums. I'll find him a nice hotel in the neighberhood.

FATSO: "On my screen, I've got New Jersey filled with water. The trolley car dead. Houses down. A bit like all of us!"

SKINNY: "That's because you've got a three day OLD beard, like one of those male models! Besides, I'm hooked on a fear of dying."

FATSO: "Imagine yourself, like the wife of a king, walking on hot coals, to see if you slept with a knight. Ok! He placed a sword between the two of you, but…"

SKINNY: "As she walked or was it him? She sang lyrics she had heard on Radio France. She dyed her hair blond. I say (and then, I added) an adventure is an adventure, don't you agree?"

FATSO: "Remember, her husband whispered! If ever I grab him or her, I'll send both to the tower to wait for the executioner. But he's on his summer vacation until the end of August."

SKINNY: "I hum a Wagnerian opera, and read one of Niethchee on Wagner. Then I'll climb up to the third floor. But, I did say to you, how I wished I could speak her language! After all, isn't that a New Year's resolution?"

FATSO: "I'D DO ANYTHING TO LOOSE MY East Berlin accent!"

SKINNY: "Did I ever tell you how I hated my third grade teacher?"

CHAPTER V


She gets up, puts on a tattered blue bathrobe. Ties it around her waist.

Her smelly bed stinks. She says how she's angry at herself, when she hears herself piss, as it dribbles down, behind a linden tree.

Then, as if she were talking to herself, she says:" Fuck all of you! When I get to Berlin, I'll tell you the truth, not until then."

In the bus, all of us wore the same color lipstick.

All of us were dreaming about what it would be like in Berlin! I said to myself, don't believe your dreams! I dreamt of a Fat- Lady dressed in red, looking over a gigantic pool!

Then somebody said: "Gute Nacht!"

To make a month's rent, I gave up most of my dreams…

I dreamt about a Weimar businessman whose

 Hand slowly walked down my back. He asked if I would

teach him my language. He said I had a special breath for my country.

Others dreamed of being photographed by Leni Riefensthal.

If I had enough money from a client, I'd take him upstairs, to the roulette room.

All that time,

 I dreamt of sitting at a sidewalk café, eating pastry.

He inhaled a Cuban cigar. Ashes fell on the floor. It reminded me of a bar with the floor scattered with ashes.

He asked me to take a bite out of his sausage.

I said: "the price list is on the side!"

The Fat-Lady in red, in her warning voice, told us, once again, about giving out free gifts!

(I heard the neighing of circus horses.)

I heard them riding in, around 3 o'clock in the morning,

I heard them setting up their tents. Getting the mike to do its work.

All my classmates were promised new clothing, and all of that, free, once we got to Berlin. And then he added: "Everything I say is a perfect truth."

A lady measured us from top to bottom, including our sweat and shoe sizes.

In the distance, I heard my father's drunken voice.

She said: "He said : Don't tell me your age!"

The bus driver yelled at us.

"If you're going to Berlin with me, now's the time to pile in!"

I thought I heard my father's voice, pumping air in my bike's front tire.

Fat-Lady in red yelled out: "Imagine yourselves in a new flat!  A window! A garden below! New clothing!! Two pairs of red shoes! And a pack of cigarettes!"

 She wore a "Buffalo Bill belt" Then, another: an "Anny Oakly!"

She hurled out orders.

"That's Berlin, for all of you!"

ENTER

QUOTE: "Keats: "This living hand…" Balthus hated narrative painting…" T.S .Eliot: "Nothing is made of naught…" Gertrude Stein: "Not not not no…" Siegfried Sassoon: "And gather me to your arms."

Georg Trakl : "Like blue water falling over rocks." Frank Kuenstler:"Should a poem have a title?"

FATSO: "What's the latest stuff you got read?"

SKINNY: "Pound's "The Age of Reading."

She, or was she a he? She walked on hot coals to prove that, in the forest, they didn't…well, you know what?

He, waiting on his mini-throne, says, "if  can't remember, then I've got enough coal to make my day!"

She looks at him, in the dewy morning. Lights filtered smoke. Disappears behind a huge linden tree. She cancels out her butt, on what she thought might be a trolley track. (It's all in the mind.) As she walks back to where he's rolling up the thick blanket, she invents lyrics to fit the occasion. It's all in her ear, he doesn't hear a thing.

She remembered how, once on a girl scout X-mas vacation, out in the close-by wilderness, she slipped and dirtied her smock. "Thank God!" Her tee shirt hadn't been touched, the one she had bought at a Sunday morning fair.

CHAPTER VI

SKINNY: "An adventure is an adventure!"

FATSO: "Stupid!"

There's an audible whisper, out here.

He said:" check her out, I mean, that blond over there. She's the perfect broad Hitler wanted his soldiers to fuck, in order to create blond men, with lots of blue eyes."

Both stare at their faces, in the eyes of the other.

Globs of sperm on his jockey shorts.

Remembrances of nights' past in the pool.

SKINNY: "Just to keep the record straight, I did walk up three flights of stairs. I thought to myself, how I wished to speak her language, to get things straight, and not just hit the sack, as they say in movies."

FATSO: "I'd love to get rid of my East Berlin accent! Otherwise, I'm a dead give-away."

ENTER

QUOTE The Raven: "Your words are silent…"

FATSO takes a deep breath: "You're doing OK!"

She waits for him to drop his cash in the box, on the left side of her table. She says, to herself, in broken German, "Now, we're right into it!"

She ambles toward the bathroom. Closes the door. Switches on the light. Sits. Hums.

 Outside, he can hear a minor water fall. She remembers, smiles at how she had crouched behind a linden tree and pissed her heart out!

Loud music.

"How long is it before we get to Berlin?"

An answer I couldn't make out. She dreams. She hums a thought, hears a Fat-Lady in red saying: "Put on purple lipstick and black eyelashes. I'll measure each one of you for a cute little skirt. When you get ready, depending on someone's dream, you'll slowly roll it up, fold it, and place it under your table."

Check his smile.

Was that a real dream?

(I heard: "Gute Nacht" Then, a sentence. That was it! My ears told me, right then and there. Otherwise, much as in an art history class, I would be informed, via my eyes, with what that really meant!)

(I heard a businessman zip down his trousers (I loved that word!) I waited for him to ask me to take off my  skirt. He came from Stuttgart, or some sound like that! He wanted the full menu. I said: "Did the Fat--Lady in red tell you what that would cost?" He replied, tongue in cheek, before his tongue licked  my ass! "

"Yes."

The two of us made such a complicated set-up, that I wished Leni Reifensthal had taken both of us back to her studio, and ask us to make ourselves at home, on the bed she used when she was totally exhausted.

We did just that.

He had spent some time near Clichy, in Paris, a walking distance to the Sacré Coeur, not far from the Café Savoyard where surrealists met.

There, one porn shop after another. A theater.  A hawker.

Did he dream I could speak broken French, like some recent Kosovo arrival?

When he finished, after he slipped on his underwear, I took him to the roulette room.

He spoke to me: "How delighted I am to have my dreams come true!"

Another.

Then another.

Then a Cuban cigar. He wanted me to get a taste of his sausage.

Then a cripple.

At no time, at no moment, was I given time to breathe.

Her voice, through a loudspeaker: "Less talk! More entertainment!"

I heard horses neighing. I heard a wooden wagon stop, when a left wheel broke.

"All of you, so-called able-bodied women, get out and push, otherwise, we'll be spending lots of time, right here!"

He yelled out, once again: "All of you,, sixteen year old girls:  Got any diseases?"

We arrived around 3:30, flush with an afternoon sun.

In a distance I couldn't see, I heard my father pumping air into the front tire of my old bike. I thought I heard my older brother, cutting wood behind our house, next to the cabbage patch where we grew it for soup.

The driver said, turning his head in our direction: "Call me Fritzl-the-Hammer. (He thought of himself as an invitation in a Wagnerian opera.)

In the room, I was told was my own, I saw a huge poster of Josephine Baker, in her banana outfit.

"The bathroom's at the end of the corridor. You'll share it with the others."

I remembered my priest, asking me if I ever have said, outloud: "Gratis pro Deo"?

I was about to tell him what my sixth grade teacher told us to memorize:

"O rage! O désespoir!"

 At that very instant, the concierge told us where we could shower, where the bathroom was…

Then she added, as if for good luck: "Ich bin ein Berliner!" And she added, "Sie sind alle Berliner."

All I wanted was a steady job.

In a commanding voice, Fritzl added:" We have another 500 km to go before we hit Berlin. You can sing,

All that kept me from crying, as I prepared my rucksack, throwing in it what I thought I might need for a couple of days in Berlin!

There goes my winter coat! It was already mid-October.

My clogs.

I dozed off in the bus.

"Ok! All of you, so-called weaklings! Get out and push!"

He screamed.

They sang their village songs. Hints of a national anthem.

I remember my mother saying, especially on Sundays:" First you pray! Then you sing in the chorus."

"Table 38! Stop mumbling!"

I didn't know my address for them to write me a post-card. I made up the Town Hall's address.


CHAPTER VII

ENTER


QUOTE: "There are several kinds here."  Simone de Beauvoir: "La cérémonie des adieux."

FATSO: "Who the hell cares! I mean, where you come from? What's your language?' And then he added: "Have I forgotten anything?"

SKINNY: "Never miss a chance to spout out all of your questions!"

FATSO: "Let me reply! A story is a story! You don't have to have footprints to get you there! If I can guess what you're going to ask me now, I've got the answer, so you don't have to open your mouth!"

SKINNY: "Get off my back!"

We were working our butt's off, when we heard sirens, lots of them, heading our way.

The Fat-Lady in red, in a quiet voice we weren't used to, said the pool was on fire and the fire brigade had just arrived.

Water rose in the pool, as it had never done before or, at least, not in post-war Berlin, and in this particular one, since they were, in Berlin, to satisfy hungry cocks.

Trucks had to be careful as they wended their way.

5 foot rocks blocked their way to the pool.

She screamed: "Sperm out all the water you can get out of those rubber hoses!"

Men screamed.

Tables emptied.

Girls drowned. Floated on their backs like wilted flowers on a pond.

My father had taught me how to swim.

I made it to the ladder, at the far end of the pool.

 Got out.

 Dried myself on one of those still-wet white towels.

You could hear half-naked businessmen, screaming in unison: "Help!"

Of all of them, only three trousers floated to the top of the water.

Tables 1-37 and then 38 floated by.

My best friends passed me by.

Dishevelled men held on to their wallets.

A couple of km on, our bus died.

Now, once in Berlin, I imagined myself shopping for a new-fangled dress, an autumn coat, stilletos,

and a funny feathery hat, and…spending at least three hours in a beauty parlor, where I

asked for highlights.

In a store window, I saw a beautiful leather hand-bag.

In a store, I saw…But now I've forgotten what I did see!

I spent hours walking, licking store windows, as I once heard a French couple say!

Too happy!

Then, out of curiosity's need, I decided to go to a psychiatrist.

He turned out to be a cross between Freud and Lacan! At least, that's what he said, as he pointed to a

leather chair, and I could see, with curtains parted, Courbet's "Birth of the World."

I thought to myself, why an old, worn-down leather chair?

One night, my mother sang what she had sung to me when I was a baby, and she said, I would, one day,

Hear the future.

Days later, three survivors asked that their moneys be reimbursed.

A Weimar millionaire got what he wanted, but, in the meantime, when I was on my back, and he

traveled down to my cunt, he taught me a couple of words in French.

"Memorize" he said, the verb "Etre," without which you might as well be non-existent!"

I did.

The next visit was on a Tuesday. I found his office on Wunderstrasse, 33.

Up a flight of stairs.

On his door: "Visits every Tuesdays between 5 and 7."

I rang.

He answered.

"Pleeze cum in!"

I did.

"Pleeze sit down un dis ledder chair."

I did.

"Vas is yur name?"

"Pleeze spel it."

I did.

"Haben yu mony in di banque?"

"Jawol!"  I said.

Then, on his leather couch, he asked me: "wat iz  d mader?"

I didn't want to go into details but, I did look at my Chanel watch, the one I had so admired in a fancy French-looking store window. In another boutique, I admired elongated heels, like tooth picks. All on KURFURSTENDAMM.

I said: "I've got to go, but I'll make an appointment with the person by the door."

Before going, I turned around, and said I had a recurring dream.

"Gut!"

In the bathroom, I stared at myself in the mirror, and asked myself, what I had to remember. Somewhere,

In my past, there must have been something that infiltrated my present. What was it? Or was I, unknown to

myself, concealing something?

(A haunting thought haunts me: when my father came back home drunk, my mother said:"Recip" and that was all, or so I heard, but he answered immediately, using her curiously Indian name: "Devyani," leave me alone.")

He did say: "Stop remembering! Iz bet fur yu!"

I flushed my pills down the toilet. Flushed. Little white things floated to the surface. Was that a symbol

of something?

FATSO: "Did it ever occur to you that, deep in the night, everything we've been saying has absolutely no

consequence whatsoever? Maybe it's all inconsequential?"

SKINNY: "Is that such a bad thing? I mean, we've succeeded in cluttering ourselves with so much shit!"

FATSO: "                                                    "

SKINNY:" Have you lost your voice?"

FATSO: "In a German film, I once saw midgets in a circus. Then I saw them again in Australia, looking for

a shrink."

SKINNY: "Did they settle in Romania or in Estonia?"

FATSO: "Don't be a shrink! Besides, when they got to Australia, they had nothing left to eat so…"

SKINNY: "I hate cannibals!"

Now, I can admit it, my five visits to Australia proved worthless! Neither the pills had any effect.

Perhaps, diarrhea…

Somebody told me to talk about the "Purloined Letter."

I said: "Who purloined it? And then, where did it go? Maybe in somebody's "purly loin?"

I quoted a poet: "The world is too much with us late and soon!" Or something, like that!"

"What about Lacan's seminar on the "Purloined Letter"?

On my next- to-the last- visit, I said to him: "when I dream, I see myself as Little Riding Hood!"

"Zer gut! Dat's a gut beginin!"

I paid him, and decided no longer to frequent his talents.

By that time, I had displaced my mother tongue. Severed it.

My real decision came on that Thursday. With all of those experiences, and lots and lots voiced, I

Took up my new position as a university instructor at The Frei Universität in Berlin. My German had improved that much!

"Why?" I asked my class, "did Samuel Rosenstock, from Moinesti, in Eastern Romania, change his name

to Tristan Tzara? Why Le club Voltaire in Geneva?  In fact, why do poets, among so many other human beings, change their names?"

Change their names?"

Somebody laughed and asked me:" is there a "rire in decrire?"

Everybody laughed, resoundingly.

QUOTE: "FATSO: Theory in Paris."

SKINNY: "Theory! Theory! Theory! What else is new?"

FATSO: "Is it true the world turns on French theory?"

SKINNY:"Just to give somebody a job!"

FATSO: "Whom do you think they're reading?"

SKINNY: "If I told you : Roland Barthes. What would you say?"

FATSO: "I say what I say!"

SKINNY: "What have you got to say, at this very moment?"

FATSO:"…and much more…!"

She says the best way to learn French is to read Mallarmé's

 "Les dieux antiques"

She adds: "Whatever is on the eye of the page, sniff it out! Don't depend on words from somebody

else's mouth! Really, if it's a painting or a poem, or worse, a piece of music, don't wait for some

authority to provide you with knowledge! If you're into it! Do it!"

She had been a part-time instructor in NY. She finished her doctoral dissertation on Eighteenth Century

Porno. novels and their illustrations. She passed with honors. She was offered a part-time position, which she

Turned down.

"I'm going back to Berlin."

Before riding from the Berlin airport, she sent a registered letter to Herr Schmaltz, telling him how she

would  love to teach Proust, and have her students cover him from cover to cover!

Shmaltz screamed.

Where were those beautiful Proustian signs, now, in her Berlin office?

She closed her eyes.

How would she ever earn a living? Where would she go? Who would  ever publish her dissertation?

She closed her eyes.

Could she become Another? A Hollywood agent? An accountant?

My father told me, a hundred times, fidgeting with his old rifle: "In battle, there's no direct road to victory!"

FATSO AND SKINNY: "Is there a space between words concealing words? Maybe, an artful space, right up our alley… besides, do  words hide words? I wonder if wondering is sufficient, especially when we chorus… All's right with proper questions. MAYBE, IT'S All in our Past…"

We know when we stop questioning our abilities to wrestle with words, but what about

Diderot's "Les bijoux…" When we read it? Well, our instructor frequents such a place. The chair wishes to visit, to see how bi-sexual ladies-men do their thing. With his book-filled eyes, can he actually see anything but his desires, on the dance floor, in the toilets, or wherever such dual company becomes one? We ask, but we do not know, except we did see table 38 take off her bathing suit, before swimming across the pool to a ladder. She murmured how her father had done…Do you remember her words? In fact, what did he actually do? As she climbed up that plastic ladder, one of many steps, near the diving board?

Would it be possible to split ourselves back into or out of our names?

Listen: "I'm doing my best! After reading a novel, for a class discussion, I dreamt I might find a diary and there, duplicate the novelist's real intentions? Besides, let me count the ways she entertained her lovers, especially the one in the carriage, going to church and…flipping up the curtain, throwing out a letter."

Authorities, at least that bourgeoisie dreaming of their sons going to the Ecole Normale supérieure, and thus assuring them of a career. In court, you could hear them breathe a sigh of relief. In a chorus, you heard the jury yell out: "To jail! For all those porno writers and illustrators!"  At 12 o'clock, the court proceedings were cut off. The judge's lunch time.

On the third floor, she dreamt of becoming a Hollywood star, playing a sexy part in a Cecil. Be.

Her mirror reflected her desires. She moved to the left, and then to the right. She lowered her green blouse.

She smirked.

She whistled.

As if she were tempting a male to join her in the bathroom.

Was she waiting for him? Was it all a visual trick? Something he made up, as he approached her? She saw him approaching through the high mirror.

They turned on the T.V.  Night goodies.

A SOCCER GAME.

Now, and without interruptions, a scripted visual on Germany's industrial might.

Now, some body-body action.

FATSO: "I saw a man, a woman, two kids."

They stared at the Senate, to the left of their address. Saw French, beautiful-bodied policemen

SKINNY          : "I WOULD  LIKE TO PROPOSE TO THIS FAMILY, a trip down south. I suggested they drove down boulevard Jean Jaurès. Pick up a Renault. Drive to highway:" A-6. Then, stop at Saumur-en-Auxois. Lunch. Three fried eggs for each appetite. Baguettes.  Butter. Then, rest at the highway station, and go on."

FATSO: "Why not the entrance at Porte d'Orléans?"

SKINNY: "Never drink a glass of Chablis. Bad…"

FATSO: "Why hadn't I been photographed, in my cap and gown, when I graduated High School?"

"While I'm in a story mood, why not undress?"

He looks aside.

He knows, or he thinks he knows

Her body.

(I can't help remembering Foucault's "The Use of Pleasure!"

HERE    goes my memory!

"The last consideration he invokes concerns lineage and the necessity of a bastardless race…"

Foucault continues: "In this problematization of relationships with adolescent boys…"

That certainly is not the

 Play with me and Skinny! We are already adults…

                                (He hears her verbalizing a Foucault memory as an illustration.)

He dreams of having his ears pierced.

(He recites ten lines from a Schiller poem.)

Looks aside.

By now, he knows her body, by heart.

Now, as I stared in the mirror, words my father told me how, just how, in battle, there are no roads Going back. Tears dribbled down his left cheek. He said he was nearly hit by a bullet, but a soldier, next to him, fell flat on his back, a bullet thru his mouth.

By that time, three years as an instructor, waiting for a promotion, despair crept in. I had, for a moment, Put my father side.

Had the chair of my department read my articles, my dissertation, with a publisher ready to consider it Publishable? It…At night, I couldn't sleep. I repeated, endlessly, how it is so difficult to fall asleep.

I tore up letters to my colleagues, the very ones in whose minds my fate depended upon.

Chapter VIII

To pass the time of the afternoon, she tried her hand at a puzzle, some friend had given her, telling her it was all Chinese!

A B C D

1 3

2 1

3

4

To answer my boss's questions, I did play with the idea of dancing in the "Indiscreet Bijoux," finding a suitable partner at night.

I saw myself walking, hand in hand, with that new German instructor, whose office was next to mine.

And thinking exactly what I had in mind, for the last three weeks. I had my ears pierced. I bought flashy Earrings. I had my nose pierced. I dreamt of something pierced, next on my belly button.

Gertrude asked me where I had all of that done.

She asked me if I knew of a pool where she might swim on Fridays, and in the neighborhood (she didn't want to take the number 96 bus, even though she had heard that there, the water was a bit warmer! (The bus stop was too close to that list of concentration camps, she knew, by heart, from Auschwitz to Bergen-Belsen.)

When she wasn't teaching, she wanted to know if all those piercings on her body would rust?

I only knew of one pool.

I didn't want to give her the address.

Every Friday, late afternoon, I'd go to the Fat- Lady in red, and take my position on table 38. Actually, When all the firemen's water had drooled away, and everything went back to a pseudo-normal business was even better than before!

Once, I remember ten men, from another neighborhood, plopping in, asking if they could commandeer The pool for a couple of hours, all for themselves. They said, if they could pay with a card, it would make Life much easier.

She asked if they were planning to use Visa.

For that occasion, the Fat-Lady in red increased the number of tables. All a matter of a momentary                Squeeze.

She made it quite clear: if they were interested in rear action, there would be an additional price.

All ten took off their shoes, and walked down the carpeted escalator.

(In a whisper, I thought, did they all have young wives and small children?)

They asked if we had a screen.

They said, for quick entertainment, they had brought with them a Harrison Freud (that's the way they Pronounced  it!) and an old Betty Grable, with Harry James, playing off screen.

Really friendly as if, for most of them, this was their second time!

I asked him if he had any special instructions.

He smiled.

He had never thought about it!

He shied away from my question.

I saw myself, once again, at the shrink's.

"Do you have a boy friend?"

"Zat's gut," he replied.

"Do you machen lober?"

("Fuck you!" I answered, under my breath!)

Did he ever suspect that I was really tempted to join the "Indiscreet" team, full time, and have some

woman

make love to me?

We called her "Mme Sex."

A youngish student had an eye on me. She went to the Chair, and said: "She touched me in her office."

I suspected many of my older, tenured profs, would have loved to do something like that! In a dream, at Best!

 Two lawyers came to my office. My computer was taken away, as if I had sent her innumerable messages, that could be used in a forthcoming trial.

Months later, not a peep.

Tongues cut.

She had been asked to go to a shrink.

I knew how pleasant that experience could be!

"Pleeze, lebt de kash und di table."

When she got to Berlin, she went to see all American movies to perfect her American.

She learned US culture, that way!

FATSO: "You forgot to zip up your pants, as in Sade's "Justine!"

SKINNY: "Thanks."

I couldn't forget what the Chair was to tell me, a few weeks later: how I was so attractive getting off the Trolley, in my black US jogging pants!

He skipped the proper verb tense.

(His office smelled of withering old age.)

She hummed the second stanza of the "Song of Roland."

A  frightening memory. A Nazi hit her, with the butt of his rifle.  Others beat them. Others…

When she was saved by Soviet troops,

they raped her multiple times.

He asked if I had ever read Christopher Isherwood in Berlin?

ENTER

Quote: "Do not expect…"

SKINNY: "Have you ever read Spinoza's "Ethics?"


Time passed by.

(Doesn't it always?)

The chair, and his lady instructor, got to Paris early in the morning, with their two identical daughters.

The two identical girls hid in 2 identical closets, wearing masks he had purchased for them at the airport.

FATSO: "Look! She's undressing!"

SKINNY: "He's doing it, too, but he's got wavy balls, flabby, waltzing, ones. He could not stop reciting Schiller.

"Schiller:" selbst nennt den Lieblingsautor seiner Jugend, Plutarch, und den Rauber Roque aus dem "Don Quixote."

Then, he took off his shirt, folded it, as his mother had showed him how to do it.

He hung his tie in the closet.

Ran back to the bed.

Was she waiting for him? Was it all a visual summon? Something he made up as he approached her?

She saw him approaching, on the high circular ceiling mirror.

They turned on the TV. Night goodies.

A soccer game.

News of Germany's industrial might.

Now, some body-to-body action.

FATSO: "I saw a man, a woman, 2 kids. They were looking at the Senate. Saw cops. Saw… Put all of that Between…then hurtle words into their eyes.

SKINNY: "I WOULD LIKE TO PROPOSE TO THIS  family, a trip down South. Drive down the Blvd Jean Jaurès, pick up a Renault. Drive to A-6 highway, stop at exist Saumur-en-Auxois. Lunch.

Omlettttte

3 eggs, a baguette. Rest.

Drive on.

FATSO: "Why not Porte-d'Orlèans?'

SKINNY: "Never drink a glass of Chablis. Bad for the Renault."

FATSO: "I would like to be wearing a  cap and gown. (A graduation present?)

"While I'm in a story mood,…"

She undresses.

He looks aside.  He knows, or he thinks he knows, her body. He hears her verbalizing an illustration, while he dreamt of having his ears pierced.

He recited a couple of lines by Schiller. He looked aside. He knows, tonight she only knows her body, Reflected in a large circular mirror on the ceiling.

However, she had read an 18th century novel.

She recited an illustration, while he dreamt of having his ears pierced. Would that make him look Slimmer in that same mirror?

He unbuttoned his US blue, button-down-shirt.

Then he threw himself on the bed,

Stared at himself in the huge circular ceiling mirror.

ENTER

QUOTE: "Al Jolson sings in a  movie."

FATSO :"Was that the beginning of your Berlin novel?"

She turned to him,and asked: "

What are you thinking about?"

She tried to recall criticism in conventional novels, all with: "He said…" "She said."

Felt like a bus ride through, as they say, uncharted minds!

I heard the driver whistle an operatic tune.

Once, he had visited Berlin for a quick fix. Once he tried walking in bombed-out neighborhoods.

What's left? Truth? A memory of the end of the Second World War? The near- death of a city, or at least, a city that was going to arise as..

Somebody, next to me, somewhere in a Berlin trolley car, said God's destruction was part of memory.

She held on to her Lutheran Bible.

I answered: "Leica, Kunst Strass. 38, 3rd floor."

"Why Leica?"

'My father's. He bought it in a fair in Poland, before the war. A clever duplicate."

I heard nothing.

"I asked: "Why  are you over- weight?"

He answered: "The Dolomites! Too much cheese! Too much Schwartzbrot!"

"At the end of the day, I took off my black bathing suit. I'd give Turkish lessons to a German Businessman, hoping to make lots of euros!"

("Listen, you'll never guess what I saw, on the corner of Heidegger and Hegel! An American captain, photographing something.

He held a tiny brown camera.

His girlfriend a huge lens.

What she was shooting at, I can't see, all I do know, buildings were no longer visible. Stuttering street Signs on the ground, where once there had been houses, probably a four story building.

SKINNY: "Iisten, FATSO! You need a pair of new glasses! I know Marx read Hegel. Did you know he also Read St. Simon, Auguste Comte, Darwin…"

(At night, she lullabied him. Tried to keep him from shouting in the middle of the night.

He remembered, with great accuracy, where he had been. He woke up with a start, and said: "Where's My uniform? My leather gloves?  My boots, just shined?" He turned over and yelled out:" Where's my Rifle?"

He said: "The Armenians were our goal!"

Mud everywhere.

He nearly choked me.

He kicked me.

His right arm rested on my right breast.

He snored with an unknown pleasure.

He sobbed.

Screamed.

"Hurrah! For our Turkification of Armenia!"

Mother said: "Don't start that all over again!"

"I was young. I studied geography at a local university!"

I saw mother washing a soup bowl.

"In Berlin, I wondered if my mother and my father had ever loved each other? Or was I a midnight Mistake?"

The night lingered on stars like candles.

Then, in a dewy morning, a rainbow…

My city brother, working on his diploma in a technical school, read Marx in his spare time.

Afterwards

AS IF SOMEBODY HAD ORDERED IT.

The city turned on its lights.

"Schiller?"

"Akhmatova."

After she died, we read her last letter. She wanted to be cremated, and thrown into the Wannsee, next to her twin sister. That sister, whose three kids now live with their grand-parents, in Karlsruhe. Before You ask,

Not one of them had joined the Party. In fact, one of my grand-parents' sister hid Jewish boys in her Cellar.

In another village, Nazis ran through the village, killing all circumcised boys, or were they denounced by Neighbors?

ENTER

QUOTE: "I've got the world on a string…"

FATSO: "One more question: What was your name? I only know you as "Chair."

CHAPTER IX

They dreamed of prosecuting a Turkish whore.

"If you sell your body's soul, you shall be prosecuted to the maximum."

He makes the sign of the cross on

His black robe.

She changed her name to Gretchen, dreamt of Faust, but with a new-found strength, she imagined Herself, waiting in the wings, ready to go down to the street, wearing a new outfit, eyes threaded.

Flowers grew, dismembered, in her delusion.

She voiced her thought, salivating: "See me scorned by life."

"Do you order me to sit on that wooden bench, facing you?"

He says: "Are you troubled by doubts?"

With both hands,

He straightens out his robe. Stares at his curled cock.

He says: "Magic will save us!"

She says to herself: "You've read too many books, and. look, your soul is sad."

She says to herself: "I've got my own reality, outside yours."

"Have you ever seen your life as a pile of used books?"

"I'm not a legal document."

FATSO: "When I was in high school, I learned how to dribble."

SKINNY: "I learned how to talk in public. Don't you think we might become a duet?"

FATSO: "I hear voices, and no one's there. But they speak in black robes."

SKINNY: "Congrats!"

FATSO: "For what? "

(SKINNY: "(YOUR WIFE HAS JUST GIVEN BIRTH TO A TOT OF A GIRL! WHAT'S HER NAME?")

(FATSO:"MOYENNE," BUT MY WIFE, THAT SWEETY DICTATOR, CHANGED IT TO:"MINNY!")

"While I went hay stacking with my father, I sweated sweetly, as a young girl may be allowed to do! Then, back home in the kitchen, with my mother, we checked out an old family album. I saw my Grand-Father, without a beard, without glasses. I saw the opera ticket he had saved: a Wagner! He walked back Home, after hitching a ride from Vienna. He wrote his trilogy! Everything he had ever dreamt of, Surfaced, as a memory of a future remembered."

"Father lit the fire in the fireplace. An ash leapt unto the rug, that beaten-old rug! now, A rug of ashes! To get our minds off the fire, my father lit his cigar. In the album, only dirty images survived!"

"At another time, but not that one, as if I lived in a double time, his smell had evaporated! Only an Identifiable one lingered on the page! A sort of a measured death as if, in time, nothing would be left in The family album!"

"A cheap perfume, out of a desk drawer!"

But grandfather had fought in the war.

As the picture talked, I could hear canons in the distance.

Bodies crumbled, one on top of the other.

Rifles spread out like autumn leaves.

Drifts of imaginary snows.

I could not escape the eye of my eyes.

At other times, I fabricated a  present.

A dog howled, just to please me.

Dyspeptic, waving a duplication.  Asking.

(The same person.)

Like a story in the wings, it was ready to walk upon an imagined stage, waiting for a massive attack of Applause--                          not heard.

"Now, I'm a now of…" Something entered my body, as if a foresight of whom I would become,
once in Berlin.

Litanies in the wings.

Arms flaying in the water, a predictable sequence rose to the surface.

I was dazzled by the French: "ETRE."

Then: "Aufklarung."

I thought I overheard that Fat –Lady in red, as a thought to be!  Eyes, I could imagine,
commanding.

Table 37: "Can't you be quicker?"

Table 38: "Can't you be quicker?"

Beneath our tables, a mock green field. Palm trees at the four corners of the pool.

I wondered if, one day, I'd meet a man fully dressed,

Roped in silver.

I wrote, while they were coming all over me:

A dream of love

The air comforts you.

Days in darkness.

# Paris:
# Truth In A Rug

## Part Two

y village shouldered me, when I left.

I heard a record of Cuban music,

Encompassing my legs.

A shallow day.

Words in a broken memory.

A world of broken sidewalks.

Leicayed.

"Please, come a bit faster! Others are waiting in line."

Shouldering my thoughts, quiet thoughts, a quiet turbulence, as if I couldn't ever get my village out of My mind, as if I couldn't stop remembering that endless bus ride!

Stop that artificial smile.

"Were those memories mine or someone else's? You warned me, table 34!"

Had I forgotten to put a stamp on everything?

"My family?"

"My dog?"

"I heard you sneezing over your barley soup. A slice of black bread next to your knife.

Were you, like my grandfather, still knee-high in some foreign land?"

FATSO: "All quiet on the middle-front."

SKINNY: "Who's watching after that baby girl?"

I was a baby, crawling under the dinner table.

Time hand-cuffed me.

On the third floor, there was a Jewish family. One night, I heard boots. A door knocked down.

I never saw

Them again.

My memory stared at my past.

"Die Endgeit ist nun gekommen.

und ich bin der, auf den…ihr

gewartet habt."

Now,                                        Gounod's "Faust."

FATSO: "Why are you whispering?"

SKINNY: "Do not ask Balthus to polaroid that baby, to turn her into a creature he desired!"

FATSO: "OK! I'll buy her a birthday cake, with her name on top, and flowers all around!"

My memory stared at me.

Others stand.

16 year old classmates

Ride wooden horses.

But, did I ever tell you: "Look! Just like the Good Old Days, the BCO (Big City Opera).

My mother loved operas. When my brother says he knows music, my mother, with a good
Sense of humor, says:

         "You smell bourgeois!" And she laughed hysterically (as she
had Never done before!)

BCO put up a large banner, opposite the church.

A voice said: "We shall be playing…" (Keeps us guessing.)

Then it added, in a chorus: "Franz Schubert (1797-1828)"

Our class, of 16 years old, applauded, even before the concert began.

We looked, intensively.

Some of us, in particular, stared at the 16-year-old-page turner and, at the end of the piece,
How the famous pianist put his arm around her!

For me, that was the proof of respect and…yes, love!

You closed in on the Truth.

Cotton candy covered my brain.

Your language is a wreck.

Afternoons.

"Out of the pool!"

"Guards:

Take her away."

Above the judge's HEAD, open orders.

Imprison her

Mind…

2 guards, in a foreign language,

Handcuff her to their flies,

Ask her if she wishes to eat something.

They listened carefully to her silence.

Coffee break, broken, ended.

They all listen to

Silence.

"Guards, take her away."

That smell overwhelms me, always the smell of burning oil,

My father's tractor.

Apples fall in autumn.

Stop those circus horses from inhaling air.

Every time in Berlin, oil trucks pass, liquidate the smell.

I imagined my mother writing:

"Please, write!"

Movie airplanes crash in fields of rotten death.

They added to the scene: gender, as a form of deflated penises.

(He ignored her falsetto laughter. Thought how his father, in the Wehrmacht, had personally
Forced a Jewish old lady, on the 3rd floor, into a waiting truck. The driver smoked an East
German cigarette.

      "You shall be voyaged to somewhere in the Atlantic." They turned to the Turkish
Prostitute: "Soon, before you know it, it'll be your turn!"

"Get up!"

"Get dressed!"

A door closes in a police station.

Panels outside.

Screams.

"Wipe them all out!"

"Get up!"

'Get dressed!"

She tries to remember what was the color of her sister's bathing suit, when she had been
Invited to Berlin, to compete in the women's 400.

(That September night, it might have been around 11 o'clock, they, too, took out their pearl-
Handled knives.

Forced the customers…                                        Knifed their asses. Forked their sexes.

Put on a Strauss waltz.

Voices overheard.

They sang, in unison: "A girl's a girl and that's that!"

I heard there were hundreds of Turkish girls in West Berlin.

"You'll be escorted to room 31 on the 3rd floor."

Floor after floor.

Corridor after corridor.

Doors, with ranks, and other names, spelled out on them.

Finally, I'm pushed into one of the darker rooms, with an iron chair, and an old desk, facing it.

Name

Address

Phone number

A smallish man, took all the information down, on a yellow pad.

"What's my crime?"

The interrogation stops on the second.

"It's now 12 thirty."

"Time for lunch."

"Have they convinced me of my guilt? As a dirty foreigner?"

Was it my face I saw in that huge mirror?

CHAPTER

ENTER

QUOTE: "O Careless! Wilt thou wilt dispatch me?"

Das Bild may send a photographer with an old Lieca.

She's asked to undress. "On your back!"

Shredded carpet.

Spots of blood.

A powerful period smell.

"You! For the time you're here, your sentence is in perfect harmony. Nazi women will escort
You to the torture chambers!"

Two years in jail, and then to Poland.

(This is Berlin, before the war.)

She whispers to herself, in her broken tongue: "I have lost my future."

But nobody will ask me about the pool.

Guards stare, smirk.

"Who shall take her first?"

"Why not all of us?"

"I'll take the back. You take the front, the lower part. You'll eat her breasts."

"When you finish, we'll switch."

"In the meantime, sing us a Turkish love song."

Smiles all around.

Songs.

Talk.

The third one, forces his prick into her mouth. Traces of lipstick remained.

"Promise you'll never utter a word, not even in Turkish!"

She shuns her memory. Confuses the judge with one of her rapists.

(Through the walls, she hears women screaming.)

There's a newspaper on the ground.

A picture of Hitler, with photographs of his favorite men:

Wilhelm, Adolph-Florian, Friedrich… Faces fade away.

"I'm innocent.

It's all Hitler's fault." (von Hermann van Harten)

(Paul Celan writes:  "The dead—still go on begging.")

There's a pool of blood on the floor.

"You see," she says, "those kids on the street? They're building make-shift bunkers, on what
Remains of the sidewalk."

They fill them with remnants of the recent past, while women stand in line to get their weekly
Milk, coffee and bread.

"They were all my students, when I started teaching, in that lower school, around the corner."

Thousands died on the Russian front.

"Why don't you take a picture of us, in the snow?"

Thousands of images reverberate in my memory.

FATSO: "You can't imagine how I'd love a hot dog with mustard, and German-made
Sauerkraut!"

SKINNY: "Around the corner, if there's still a corner! But you've got to stand on line!"

In a dim light, she remembered the last Soviet Lt. before he left. He lectured me on the need
for a future, or was it "A" Future?

He spelled it out: SOCIALISTICHESKI.

He wept.

Nazi troops, in a village, gathered young boys near a wall and knocked off their heads.

ENTER

QUOTE: Georges Bataille: "Conclusion."

Now, it was Saturday, May 19th 1945. Others, in that same Polish village, saw me, and wondered if I could give them a blond descendant?

Father never uttered a word, happy to cut the sausage, and drink the local brew, and tell us how many Armenians he had killed, as if we had a failed memory. Then he stopped.

Kissed me.

A knock at the kitchen door.

A Nazi captain entered: " Bring your daughter, now!"

Mommy hadn't the slightest idea of what that request meant.

I came into the kitchen.

He took me away.

I was supposed to go to the Eastern Front, facing Stalingrad.

In front of me, a makeshift tent. 20 soldiers inside, singing a Nazi song.

I could hear zippers sliding down.

I was ordered to enter.

A Russian voice, in a terrible German accent!

"Me, first!  Then, the rest of you, ā la Russian,

Fucked me."

It was a freezing night.

("Now, it's your turn.")

(It's all in the rhythm.)

The tent's curtain flapped open.

"Dad, after all these years, may I still call you 'Dad'? Like the other kids in my class?"

"Let me send you a picture postcard of my neighborhood in Berlin! And here's my address…"

Father replied: "Do you live in a Turkish neighborhood, like Kreuzberg, surrounded by

headgears…

Next to a Turkish pastry shop?"

Now, I've got a new vocabulary, a new geography. I now know how to find my ways in Berlin! My truth!!

My father's got limited vision: he's always talking about how many Armenians he killed in one day. And The great meal he had that night! Then he smiled, and added: "I'll never forget all of that! Never!"

Time flashes back.

I can hear repetitions.

 A circling wheel.

Screams. Pop corn. Hot dogs.

Cotton candy.

SKINNY: "I dream of an endless Intermission…Got anything to fill in the blanks, while people hurry to the Male-female johns?"

FATSO: "Poetry translates Greek into German, into English!"

Only I

In the dark

My sliced tongue

Underneath my skin

Words disappear

SKINNY: "Now's my turn:

Forgot the first line, too bad!"

What would my family say, hearing my new vocabulary? Again, I hear him verbally fighting in Armenia! Sometimes, I hear a cynical voice. I hear firefighters trying to put out a huge fire in East Berlin. His head wavers over the table, before falling on the table, but he says "repetitions." He continues, his eyes dark and damp. He recites a childhood ditty:

Lost at sea

An ice-dream wrapper floats by

I fictionalize the future: quiet now, and heard underwater skiers.

I slithered.

Sounds of micro-shifts of helpful zippers.

Memories in the darkness of an amusement park.

"Most of them were French"

Mark Holloway, "Heavens on Earth"

(Dover Publications Skimming noises.(Dover Publications. Inc,NY) p. 204

A side wall flickers. An automatic row-boat slithers below Niagara Falls.

Girls scream.

Boys slide their hands where they shouldn't be.

Now, a throw of the dice… guess the end!

At that moment, I hear myself thinking, just to get my mind off the poem.

A recollection of war-words:

"Take a picture of me, leaning against that invisible wall."

A Japanese  instructor, in the next classroom, with an insisting voice says:

"All is Langage!"

She notes, in her quadrilaterally,-lined schoolbook, what she's heard: "I warned you!"

"If it turns out, they don't exist, you lose your wager, then God exists, then, you'll get a
free free pass to Florida, to the Castle Hotel, with the largest kidney-shaped pool outside

Hollywood!"

SKINNY: "A few Nazis survived. Brandenburg survived.  A treasured pool survived."

"Did truth survive?"

FATSO: "It's all in the mind, as a famous …"

SKINNY: "Go on…"

FATSO: "I can't."

SKINNY: "You must!"

FATSO: "Sounds like dialog in a play!"

All the above came out of an imaginary dismissal of truth! But, if the lights were to dim, actors could be Part of a Scene, their mouths open. But they've all fled from sight, under a barrage of silent applause. A Rehearsal cancelled. The cast, including the director, the stage manager, electricians-- they all went for a Midnight pie-ā-la-mode.

Most wanted Apple, others preferred Blueberries.

Under a bluish sky, memories evoked memories. She heard champagne corks pop into the scattered ceiling paint. Still, on the floor, yesterday's old school books. A smattering of wisdom!  She could hear, On the 4th floor, a hand-wound phonograph with Maurice Chevalier singing.

She heard water swimming away.

She heard fire-engines.

She saw huge fire hoses drowning the pool.

To understand them, she said to herself, you need to find answers to Edmond Jabès's "Book of Questions."

She said to herself, I should have bought a brand of New Year's Eve, noise-makers, to knock out the Noise.

She knew ghosts would not deny their ideologies.

She remembered how her mother would say, at Christmas, "be careful when you light the candles on the Christmas tree!"

Two years ago, one of the candles flickered. A branch caught fire. They say that our next door neighbors saw our house blow up in flames.

We waited for the fire brigade to arrive, rubber hoses they had used as an interrogation method. She heard herself scream, in a gestapo hotel. She was asked, with severity:" Who are you?  Where do you live?  Phone number? How many of your Neighbors could vouch for her? Had she ever been secretly tempted to be tortured on the fourth floor, Below Gestapo headquarters?"

She caught sight of herself in a forest of words.

For a moment, she thought of Tristan und Iseult.  Ghosts slipping under the door, speaking Armenian, With a touch of royal English, probably come down from some ambitious French nobleman.

She said to herself:

"Let's celebrate the Unknown!"

In Prague,

All restaurants have trilingual menus, to avoid public altercations.

After the pool emptied, she found herself walking through memory. She bought herself a fancy watch, hoping, by turning the dial backwards, she might, mysteriously, find herself back in her kitchen. She saw her mother baking bread.

 She heard her father snore.

She cleaned up the dust, underneath the dinner table.

She heard disemboweled sounds yet, simultaneously, clanging bells of a passing trolley car. She walked down a muddy street with her Leica, shooting the past as past: what was left of it.

Rubble, all around her, rubble. The smell, out of a Turkish restaurant, with left-over food, dribbling down into the gutter.

A boy's voice: "Watch out! Parts of that roof may come down on you!"

His friends huddled.

They whispered: "How much?"

"My dear captain! Tell me about your past! I've already talked about my own."

"My parents came from tsarist Russia, in the suburbs of Odessa.

When they reached Ellis Island, their name changed from Boltonowsky to Bolton. They had escaped a slow pacing death.She asks: "What was it like in Odessa? Did your parents ever talk about it?"

Isaac Babel writes: "Odessa is a horrible town."

"We moved to Hester Street, in a one-room apartment, with one light in the kitchen.

The kitchen Table. That's where I did my homework. That's where I memorized my Hebrew lessons. My mother read The Last canons of the Old Testament:"

Our next door-neighbor said:" Next year in the Bronx!"

The Torah, and within it, Genesis, Exodus, Leviticus, Numbers, Deuteronomy. My father reminded all of Us, around the kitchen table (we had nowhere else to sit down, in what we called our living room, when we rented it.)

Mother stopped my Father.

She looked around,  at all of us, and smiled.

 She hoped one more son would become a rabbi, and another one, the boy with a beautiful voice, whom We heard singing in the shower. (Mother remembered, and we never forgot it, that, in the old days, Showers were taken in the kitchen, in a large brown bucket, filled with lukewarm water poured, on us. Sometimes, even washing our hair in it. There, he sang. "A future cantor," she would say!

"In the Torah, the first human beings were mentioned.  That is, a family, the history of the Jewish people. That was the beginning of the history of a family, the beginning of ours.

Mother stopped.

She looked around our small dinner table, and she was sure our family must have been like the very first One. We went to synagogue, around the corner, on Holy Days, when the men wore sneakers! She also knew the larger portion of a heritage (if ever we could do that!) would be given to the oldest boy. That Was me.                    Every year, she would say, our family follows the Torah.

Out of our building, next to poverty, we walked to synagogue, right around the corner. No one can forget the Sabbath!

She had been told, by her father, of members of a Jewish sect (the word horrified me!) mourning Over The Destruction of the Temple. Father interrupted, and said how he would have wanted to belong to an Ascetic movement among the Karaites, in Jerusalem.

Mother would add her own translation of the Haggadah, which included the very thing in talmudic Literature.

She looked at me.

I said, in a serious voice, that the Love of God had been described by Maimonides.

Then the meal. Better than our Hebrew National!

(It took a long time to discover what father did, when he said he worked off 5<sup>th</sup> Avenue, in the diamond Dstrict. But we learned (how?) he was paid a miserly salary, as a broom sweeper, after closing hours.) I remembered how he loved a glass of manischewitz . After a glass, he drank one more, until his head was about to slump down, on the kitchen table. At that instant, mother would tickle his neck, and he would jump up, slowly. But then again, he started talking about his death and, looking at me, the eldest Son:  he said "You won't inherit a thing." Mother said: "The life we lead is a hem! Perhaps all of what we Did was to live through clothing!" We sweep away the cobwebs of our past, as quickly as possible!

ENTER

QUOTE: "If you want a metaphor, ring twice."

Every morning, my mother would give us, going to school, a peanut butter- grape jelly sandwich, on Wonder bread.

"Wash your hands when you finish eating."

That night, something unexpected happened. I said to my sister: "Why did you slide your tongue into my mouth?"

She answered: "I need practice."

That afternoon, when I got home, mother was smiling, holding a letter, and I could see a red crown on the top, and she said: "You got into Columbia College, with a full scholarship!" She kissed me on both cheeks. When father came in, I told him. He looked at me, quizzically, and said he had recently read in The Forward that the president of the University had called the chair of the English department and said To the Chair: "You've got your Jew Trilling! Now, that's enough!"

Mother was nervous. She looked at me, and said: "Be careful! You'll be in Harlem." I said I'd get off the Number 1 subway at 116th Street and walk through the campus, until I'd reach Hamilton Hall. There, in Room 301, I'd sit and listen to my professor of Philosophy lecture on many topics. At the end, he'd look Around and say: "Any questions?" A hand went up. "Yes," followed by a question. Professor Frankel Replied: "That's a very good question:

"Any others?"

You asked me what's Wonder Bread, and I replied, with a grin, "It's got nothing like your schwartzbrot."

My mother always turned to my younger brother, the one who sang, when she poured water out of a Wooden basin to wash his hair. She said: "With that voice of yours, you're a ready-made cantor!"

My younger brother, the one who would become a famous cantor on 5th Avenue! said, in a sing-song Voice, that he had read Yosef Hayim Yerushalmi's "Freud's Moses."

"Stop!"

My father said: "In this house, no Freud!"

I whispered: "Moses and Monotheism" was really a controversial and a mysterious work and that Yerushalmi was a brilliant writer, a brilliant thinker and a brilliant voice in Judaism, and he found his Place in Columbia's department of Religion.

My younger brother quoted Ludwig Wittgenstein.

My next younger brother asked my mother, was there anything she remembered about Odessa.

She said the "smells"!

"You couldn't walk down any street, without smelling coffee, spices, sausages and music!"

My sister turned her head. In the street, somebody talked rapidly about the same things, but she Remembered clothing stores, the ones that looked like the ones on Hester.

"What about Balthus?" (That question came out of nowhere) Nobody had ever heard of him.

"Don't let him paint my younger sister, with her legs apart, and a little cat at her side!"

Mother and father hated such talk, and said so.

They much preferred Chagall's cows.

I, myself, had a copy of Balthus' brother, Klossowski, and his drawings—dirty ones. (My sister borrowed them, in secret.) She said to herself, she felt my breasts growing. She had heard the French call them strawberries! In secret, she touched herself. Images crept into her dreams, and she smiled in her sleep.

In the morning, she found a pillow between her legs.

(A copy of TheTales of Genji and…no sex, there.) Mother came into her room (all of us shared the corner of one room.)

My older brother broke in, in semi-darkness. He touched himself, after having seen Klossowski's Lucretius and Tarquin.

She knew that, during the night, sometimes, she panted, when she touched herself, under her light Green blanket.

Mother kissed us all.

Turned off that single bulb.

Saturdays.

My father and his three sons (me!) walked to synagogue.

Every Saturday, we learned, again and again, what followed Genesis.

Was I dreaming?

I heard my father telling me to recite Proverbs.

I closed my ears, and repeated to myself, the authors I most admired in my Humanities course:

AristotleBerkeleyBolzanoBrentanoCohenFrischein-KCohenHilbertHumeHusserlKantKulpeLip
ps

And so, so, many others!

I especially gloated over Ludwig himself, in his Blue and Brown Books, when he wrote:

"This is a pencil"

"This is a round"

"This is wood"

(Words is me?)

The captain now added that, in a street, not far from a friend, there was the longest pool in Western Europe, around the corner, on Handel and Bismarck, where friends of his went swimming every Thursday Night.

FATSO: "Was that your first fuck? Did you keep your shirt on? Were you thinking about something else?"

SKINNY: "Are you talking to me? All I saw was a woman who looked, in her blue swim suit, like an Olympic swimmer! I heard her say, to herself:" I'm getting too fat! Somebody told me to do a low fat and low calories diet.

I tried,

And, 2 weeks later, I was right back to where I started!"

"Then, did I tell you? Immediately after Hitler killed himself, in that bunker, not far from here, I had to Stand on line, to get something to eat, something to put on.

                                    A pillow and, when I was lucky, a blanket!"

I told my parents that I had medical insurance, a paid vacation, and a retirement pension. All of that, Right after the end of the war!

 I dreamt of a winter coat.

Dreamt of my home-town sausages, that perfume, streaming through our village on Sundays, when everybody was in the village, streaming out of mass, I mean, women, while the men talked, drank and, sometimes, danced in clogs, singing old songs.

When I got to Berlin, I jumped off that bus. Somebody looked at me, and said I should repeat what he would say:

"Ich bin ein Berliner!"

"What about those black eyelashes?"

"I made myself as sexy as Marlene (she whispered to herself: "Did I get that spelling right?")

 All of that, to please that Fat-Lady in red.

She told me, quickly, how much they would be charged.

 What I had to do.

And lots of other smaller things, to please male customers who came to my table.

Once in a street, I heard children's voices, a loud voice, proclaiming:

"Are you die Frau Fucker?"

No reply, on my part.

He joked. "I think you're hiding some gut brot in dat bag!"

Out of nowhere, he asked me if I knew how to swim.

"My father taught me when I was 8."

(I dreamt of eating an apple, off-season!)

Then, one day, a total surprise for me, I heard my father had been fired as a town volunteer firefighter.

He came home. He had a rare tear in his eyes! I guess that reminded him of a much more pleasant time when he had been drafted. in the German army, to help forbid people from jumping off a long cattle Train. One of the German officers repeated what he had learned in school, in his French class:

"O temps suspends ton vol…"

"When I met you, I didn't want to tell you the truth, the whole truth, and so I played with my Leica, shooting everything in front of me, high and low, some at close range, others far-away. Sometimes, I held my Leica, in such a way, that I took a picture of myself, in a big mirror.

I said to myself, it's a mystery. Leica does its tricks, all by itself.

I snapped a torn poster of Hitler, without his head.

"Sholem!"

Someone said and I repeated:

"Sholem!"

(I told him, I had a recurrent nightmare. I saw myself, on the morning of 26 August, at Bourget-Drancy, on a train going to Auschwitz, with 15 year olds out of 365. I saw myself as one of the fifteen year olds. I told  him, I went to the Berlin station, out of fear and a horrible curiosity.)

In my classroom, I said there hung a huge portrait of Hitler, against the side window, and a couple of lines, taken from Nietzsche's "Beyond Good and Evil."

My teacher raised her arm, and said to all of us, "Raise your right arm and repeat after me:

"Long Live Hitler!"

CHAPTER

FATSO: "How much do you remember?"
The headmaster asked all the girls to form a line, and enter his office, one by one, and then he slipped his hand inside our panties. He suggested two girls fondle each other, as he photographed  them.

 He put his finger in his mouth.

Two girls were expelled.

I wanted to hide myself.

See my vision.

(I had a terrible dream. My family took me to a haircutter. I sat in a huge chair, facing a huge mirror. The Barber cut off my hair, in small snips. I saw my hair fall to the ground. An elder lady, with a broom, cleaned, at certain intervals, my hair on the floor. I saw my left eye held up by two small sticks, all the while

He cut my hair.)

"You asked me if I had heard anything?"
"Yes.  I heard boots storming up the stairs, to the fourth floor, where I knew there was an elderly Jewish Lady, living alone. Husband died three years ago.

I never

saw her again."

He asked if it hurt the first time?

When I got out of the bathroom, I stepped out of a half-filled bathtub. Then, for no reason, I could figure out, I heard my teacher asking all of us, to write down a couple of sentences, the way Hemingway had done it.

Then, I asked myself, as I tried to write, as simply as possible, but as convincingly as I could, what's Imagination for? Could it be a question of sentences? Or paragraphs?  Should everything one wrote be Autobiographical? Even, as I said to myself, what initially appeared as woven out of the imagination Itself. Was it truly about yourself? Somebody had once written: "We know, and do not know, what it is to suffer…" I agreed, when I finished my Hemingway sentence!

I covered the lenses of my Leica.

All pictures are real.

On holidays, I took pictures of anyone sitting at a table. Maybe, later, someone might want to identify Those sitters!

(My Leica slept next to me, under my pillow.)

I never thought I would become the woman I met in the street, A prostitute, of no interest.

And yet,

We sang old school songs in Turkish.

She told me there were at least 30 or forty others, working close by. She added, nobody knew how to swim, except me!

I heard again, and again, her voice:

"Ladies, get ready, the first batch is about to go down to greet you!"

I had already heard her say that, the first ten times, that it would hurt, but the money was good, so close your eyes, and do your best!"

Remember,

You're all professionals, even though you've just begun."

"Did you have other dreams?" The captain asked.

CHAPTER

I hummed a tune.

I said: "That's from 'Meet me in St. Louis! Louis!...'"

He finished the line:

"meet me at the fair."

Then a Juror popped in, with a naked question:

"How come you live in a movie world?"

I answered:

I do not…

I have not…

LET ME ADD…

The judge disguised himself in his black robes, and requested I double-check my answers:

I do not…

I have not…

LET ME ADD…

"That's better."

The trial ended, promptly at 2: o'clock.

(I couldn't forget my chance meeting. Actually, we got together, that night, and he said he knew of a Great place for us to relax. He took me to see the largest pool I had ever seen! The lapping water, all mechanically controlled! What a delight! For some reason, I thought it had cleaned my memory…A Fat-Lady in red, asked me, exactly, what I had in mind or, should I say, in body?

"Captain, Oh, my Captain, can I call you Captain Dreyfus? Devil's Island may be Berlin for you!"

The Captain answered : "My younger brother, Moishe, had just graduated from Yeshiva U. He took a whole semester, on French 19th century anti-Semitism. So, let me, here, and now, translate Dreyfus into A famous victim of French Military Justice, and Christian hatred of Jews (read the Catholic paper, La Croix, and, for Republican atheists, Aurore). You do remember how military justice was finally reversed, And Dreyfus reintegrated in the army with a promotion."

"Captain, tell me a bit about his family, so I can see where the whole thing began!"

The Captain replied: "The family came from Alsace. A nice Jewish family, who might have lived in Park Slope in Brooklyn, and have a week-end home near potato fields in Sag Harbor."

 "Ok.! Thanks! It's getting slightly clearer, but why was he condemned to Devil's Island?"

The Captain answers:

"You know, the French army lost, drastically, in 1870, and so it did anything to justify what they thought might have been an act of treason, especially, if it pointed a finger at a Jew, working in General HQ."

So, it was proven with false documents.

He was finally found innocent, and, so ended a horrible anti-Semitic moment in 19th century French anti-Semitism. (

Later, repeated under Petain's Vichy… Here's another statistic: "Les 11, 400 enfants juifs déportés de France."

P.S. If you need more info read Irene Nemirofsky.

"OK! So then, what happened?"

The Captain's answer: "A great French novelist, Emile Zola, wrote for "L'Aurore," a devastating critique of French Justice, titled:

"J'accuse!"

HIMSELF, CONDEMNED TO A BIG FINE, AND A POSSIBLE JAIL SENTENCE.

By the way, can you come up with an American novelist who might have stuck out his neck that way?"

"How about Norman Mailer…"

"Now that I've got all that info, let's have a glass of German white wine!"

CHAPTER

A juror came up with an undressed question: "Why do you live in a cinematic world?

Or, maybe, a literary one…"

But you've already read the answer:

"I…"

"You might have underlined the following:  why fool around with a semantic approach to Justice?"

"Do you know her?"

(Next question): "What was she doing in Berlin, immediately after the war? How did she earn her Living?"

She refuses to answer, but, on the spur of a moment, she answered that she loved Greek art in Turkey.

She did say something, like the following, to satisfy their curiosity.

She said:

"Time was cut like a fisherman's bait."

Now the judge:

"Save us from such pathos, worm or no worm! Does the jury actually believe she lived a well-ordered life, as a newly arrived Turkish immigrant?" (Under his breath, the judge remembered that Turkish immigrants had been burned to death by neo-nazis, in their rooming house.)

A question addressed to the judge: "Do you believe what she's been saying on the witness stand?"

She was thinking about the possibility of a two-fold answer.

"Do you believe you're living a lie in Berlin?"

(She found it easy to separate her professional life from the one she kept in her head.)

A juror's question: "What are your thoughts concerning Heidegger (minus Hanna Arendt)?"

Her answer: "I believe every German should memorize: "Being and Time." The title itself musically underscores his absolute truth."

THE JUDGE INTERRUPTS

"For you to know Absolute Truth in Berlin, must you first harbor negative truths

THE JUDGE ADDS:

"What has epistemology got to do with this trial?"

ENTER

QUOTE: "Dorothea Tanning: "What I knew all the time…"

She sits in the witness box, playing with a lock of hair, sometimes licking a curly end. She bites the skin off the left side of her thumb.

A Juror: "Let me continue, with a question that seems to me, to follow right after what I see you doing to Your Thumb…Do you believe the battery should be changed in your electric toothbrush? Or in your Vibrator?

Let me forewarn you, any wrong answer to my question might augment your prison term."

She thinks to herself: "To let my heart feel better, I'd like to hear James Taylor and Carly Simon sing Together."

Then she added: "When I was dropped off, by the circus manager, on a dark street, in what had recently Been East Berlin, not far from that massive jail, where the enemies of the Third Reich were sent: Criminals, homosexuals, gypsies, and especially, Jews.

In my thoughts, I saw myself, with a large shovel, helping my father clear out the snow, in front of our house. Such thoughts had nothing to do with 19th century French Poetry and poetics. (She laughed to herself.)

A Juror asked: "Why is she laughing?"

She sang a childhood ditty her mother had sung to her when she was a baby.

Sing to me in black

On the edges of night

Nowhere a threshold

Transparency of nothing

Absence everywhere

No mirrored reflections

A distant story

A fraudulent dance

A spark of existence

On an empty stage.

Could any poem actually reflect an inch of reality?

An elderly Berliner threw an insult in her direction: ”Filthy foreigner! Go home!”

The Fat-Lady in red swept the carpet. Nobody saw her.

She heard neighing wooden horses.

A dictionary nurse wiped the sweat off the driver's forehead.

“Has the jury reached its verdict?”

“Not yet, your honor.

We're split on that question. Could we hear, once more, her testimony as to her arrival in Berlin?”

Two jurors, from Westphalia (where they make good salami) asked for a lunch break, and the time needed to the toilet, to relieve themselves.

The Judge: “Take her away to a holding cell.”

Now she reads Das Bild.

Her attention focuses on American politics.

"Nuts," she says. "Those crazy politicos don't know what to do to get things straightened out!" On the Third page, she reads that a Balkan country is about to have a major street show of force, asking for an increase in salary for all teachers in the country. She imagines she can hear the crowd getting bigger and bigger, and the police lined up, with their heavy sticks. People, in the village, had barricaded  themselves, in wooden planks, on their windows. You could hear a crowd, coming from another direction, yelling for oil companies to lower their oil prices:

"Our tractors can't move!"

Another suggestion, this time a bit more pacific, ā la Thoreau. With their wagons, they encircled the Enemy, like they did in the good-old days, when covered wagons did the same.

Some insisted US Marines should intervene.

 Lobbyists rallied in the corridors of Congress.

"We paid for your election! Now's the time to thank us and…our companies!"

"What's to be done?"

"Too Marxist!"

"Let our good will Texaco come to the rescue."

"Who are you?"

"How long have you been in Berlin, and, to do what?"

 "Undress!"

A huge lady in a white outfit, sticks her fingers up her vagina, to find out if she's hiding something.

"Just checking!"

Two guards lick their chops. "She's ours!" They exclaim.

"Can I get dressed?"

Somebody, with a high school education, pops up with a jewel of a comment:

"Circumsize the son of Sultan Ahmer III."

Not another word could be either read nor heard.

"Why Berlin?

Finally, tell the jurors the whole truth!"

Soldiers go through Stasi underground files, trying to discover if she had ever been seen by the police, eating a sausage, with lots of Westphalian bread, on the corner of Lessing and Goethe.

A juror says: "Can't, for the life of me, eat those rotten pigs' feet."

Another says: "Sehr Gut!"

And wipes his mouth with an imaginary handkerchief.

Three guards applaud, tired out in the Stasi coffers .

"Eyes dilate"

Soon, buses would stop running.

They see a double-breasted British raincoat.

"How they'd like to crack a hard boil egg on somebody's head!"

In their lockers, they tore up the Marquis de Sade's novels and plays, and some of those wunderbar Illustrations!

"What about Xian-pottery soldiers? They'd do a much better job with that whore!"

(Strings of thoughts come at intervals.

They musicalize the page!

And, for example, what follows:

"What would happen if NCIS went without a staircase!")


Eyes dilate

                      No car fare

                      An absent sale of indulgences


                      A future child in an ice-box

"Can you sing?"

"Yes, I can!"

She sings.

She begins elsewhere, with an early:

                    "La défense d'aimer."

Her guards do not understand…

She tries out her Wagner:

"Die liehibeis Sourbrot"

Guards knock their heads together.

"What the hell's she's singing?"

They've got nothing, except, in their constant memory, a memory of an expression that inserted itself in Their brains:

"It's all the fault of those damn Jews!  O! those Jews never stop with their singing!"

Could a woman have remembered all of that?

In any case, in the "Indiscreet Jewel," Lucy and Helen danced, whispered in each other's ear. Pushed their bodies, up against the other.

"Who wrote 'thought' in a dialog?"

A guard says: "You've got a couple of seconds left, and please, do not quote one of our German Philosophers!"

Then they bring her a tray of food and add: "Weren't you a Turkish prostitute, working late hours at Mme Fat-Lady in red's space?"

She answers: "I know how to swim. My father taught me."

"Four weeks ago, I left my employment. Then, I wandered the streets of Berlin, a place to be Re-discovered, which I did, first as an instructor in the French department, then, or was it simultaneously, meeting a US Captain, on a Berlin assignment.

With him, began my third life. Or could I say my fifth                 or  sixth?

A Turkish adolescent, a prostitute, a university person, and now, a friend of an US Army captain with his Baby-Browny, and me, with my father's Leica, and now, picked up by Berlin justice, awaiting the results of my trial."

………………………..

Somebody remembered the 1936 Olympic Games, when a US black won his race. Hitler went bananas but since his "Heil" was not convincing enough, Leni asked him, and his overly be-heavily medaled Generals, to come to her studio, where she could ask them to raise their "Heil" once more, and then the Picture could be sent to every German newspaper, magazines…

In the meantime, in a Hollywood club, in Morocco, Humphrey Bogart and Lauren Bacall, and a little piano player, and a bartender, shocked the room when they sang the "Marseillaise," right in front of Nazi officers.

How many thoughts hid in the background of my memory?

I wore boots, going to school, singing a Turkish popular song with my girlfriends.

My father's head fell on the table. My mother tickled his neck.

She said: "You've got to sweep up the dead leaves in the back yard."

That may be the reason, after my life changed so radically, and so many times, that I really couldn't write back to my parents. In any case, my own memories were so many, so dense, so varied, that I really couldn't say, even to myself, what I had done, what I wanted to do.

In my dream, I presented my passport to an officer. It showed my face, the date of my birth, where I was Born, when my passport had been issued and where…So many questions remained in the dark. In fact, As I said to myself, that may explain so many things I couldn't remember.

He asked a young hotel midget to carry our luggage to our room, on the third floor, overlooking the snow-covered Austrian Alps.

Next morning, for breakfast, in a dining room with elks on the wall, and, in another part of those same Walls, old pictures of the Alps, and climbers ready to sky down velvety snow.

"Bitte, café mit schlag und jam!"

All came rapidly.

We were alone in the dining room.

Others came in later, and then, took a horse and buggy ride to go visit the nearest village to buy Souvenirs: climbing sticks, hats, and leather shorts.

(Looking up at that white-covered mountain, I wanted to be that tall, that high, as tall as a "yes," but the Earth called me. Would my whole life have been different, had I not been bused to Berlin? Yes, the further away from the predictable, the happier I was, and that's not saying, I hated my family! The bus sang popular songs, all of us knew by heart! I saw, in my eyes, a white mountain with lots of skiers fleeting down.

That night, I heard the name of all the girls who had worked with me on tables 1 through 37.

Sounds of a fire truck's whistle.

I moved from side to side. I had to go to the toilet.

He budged and said: "Where're you going?"

He undressed.

I undressed.

He took the right.

I took the left.

We shared one of those banana-shaped pillows.

"Hold me," he said, in a melancholy voice.

We heard another conversation, through the wall.

"The snow was as high, as that picture on the wall, above our heads. I heard my father's voice:

"I held my revolver in my right hand. I thought I had killed a Russian soldier to death. We were in front of Leningrad.

It was very cold, that winter."

In my head, I heard: "Get out of your sleeping bag."

He moved towards me. I eyed him from the left.

Shortly, thereafter, he got up, and madly started looking for his tie.

He knotted his tie.

Both of us came out, with the same words:

"All who exit, beware!"

Uncertain readings, going back to god-knows a "when" actually existed, or had it been a way of Sidelining Reality?

Could it have been the sun blinding me?

Snow pierced and melted in the sun.

Ski poles slipped on the snow.

A distant village clock sounded the hour.

We read the headlines in a local paper:

"A Turkish prostitute was hacked to death by neo-Nazis."

He added, to what he had already told me. After his wife's death, on the autobahn, he had inherited a sum of euros-- good for trips, clothing, food in fancy restaurants, vacations to places he had never been: like a mountain village in Austria.

How he had taken care of his daughter, after her mother's death.

I sat in the back of my favorite club, drinking.

In the chair's office, with my legs slightly apart, he said that, after hearing my story and my passion for 19th century French poetry and poetics, with a little bit of a Roland Barthes' semiotics thrown in, I appeared to be a perfect hire, as an instructor, for a limited time. His voice underlined the last part of his Speech.

A week later, I sent him my new professional address:

French dept.

U of B

Barnstrasse 42

Berlin, Germany

(I sent the same to my parents

To calm their nerves.)

A quick reply, on a post-card, with the Blue Mosque on one side and a message on the other:

"Dearest Daughter, how sad my news. Your Dad took down his rifle, above the fireplace, and shot himself in the mouth. He died instantaneously. I cleaned him up before the burial. A terrible funeral! An open pit. A priest, in his garment. A policeman. Farmers he had known. The sky had lost its clouds.

Somebody said: "Good Morning, Mrs of the Deceased. Hope you're well."

Your mother who loves you very much."

"We planted cherry trees around his grave."

Friends took lots of pictures of the funeral wreaths. Bouquets thrown on to his coffin.

It rained all night, the day of the funeral.

Four men slowly lowered the coffin, into the wet ground.

Mother dropped five German coins in the open grave.

The tombstone darkened.

Dead leaves swirled about it.

Someone cried out: "Long Live Turkey!"

Mother cleaned out the bedroom, to get rid of his smells.

Somebody, next to her, recited a line of poetry: ..."and I've been to all graves."

I wondered if mother had ever seen a film by Buñuel? She would have admired a country scene, where a magician, wand in hand, touched a coffin, and out came a guy!

A bell rang out a funeral theme from the village church.

I should have asked my friends to videotape the event.

(Here's a flashback: "I looked out the window of our Paris window, down rue Vaugirard, and I didn't see a single one of those electric chairs helping invalids move about. Nothing on the East Side. I saw hundreds of walkers on Broadway, and not a single one on Rue des Ecoles. I saw countless canes everywhere in Paris. The same on Broadway.)

FATSO: "I'M WILLING TO LISTEN, BUT I HAVE TO INFORM YOU..."

SKINNY: "Why in capitals?"

By the time I got back to my third floor maid's room, with a tiny window, overlooking those famous Parisian roofs, I heard a Roma maid vacuum clean the corridors. She had already brushed the toilet with remnants of shit from my diarrhea roommate, in the other room.

(The chair of the department mulled over what constituted a novel. He took down, from his extensive shelves, a mix of US and Fr. novels. He stuttered through unwritten novels to discover if they practiced a DADA surprise or, if they had long, complex paragraphs.

What truly irked him, was envisaging critic's response to the unusual, the unpredictable, the switches in typographical letters, and surely, the unexpected intrusion of references to movies, poems, streets, behavior, rapist jailers, etc. etc.)

She guessed she made no impression on the Chair, skimming through a mix of French and american novels.

In the university kitchen, you could hear cooks talk, waiters waiting, waitresses hovering over tables to check out the size of their tips. A wave of the hand tried to call one of them over. "The potatoes are cold!" Another read the dessert menu, and asked for a banana flambé. "Sorry. No! One of us, yesterday, got burned in the kitchen preparing that!"

She heard the plunger floundering in the toilet bowl.

Chairs scratched the floor.

Somebody, waiting, quoted a French poem:

> The flesh is triste

> And I've read all those romans.

Then, in my mind's images, I saw the Statue of Liberty roast French tourists.

Was all of that

 A shadow of reality?

He mumbled to himself.

He cried into the banana pillow.

She heard the wooden wheels of a carriage, carrying her father's body to his grave.

He nibbled my left nipple.

His tongue woke me up.

He ejaculated on my nipple.

She moaned, artificially.

She hummed an Ella Fitzgerald:

"You're my everything."

She whispered to herself: "That should do it!"

In his dream, he saw himself elsewhere.

"The flesh is weak…"

FATSO: "Check her out!"

SKINNY: "You, first."

A while later, walking out of the Luxembourg Gardens, they ambled down the street of a forgotten name, bought a bagful of cherries, washed them in a courtyard's fountain, then went walking until they reached the Seine.

The Louvre on the other side.

 The next day, they decided to sit at an outside table, at the Rostand, and check out famous people walking by. They made them up:

"There goes a famous one."

The other said: "……….."

Passers-became names.

Francis Ponge

Follain

Guillevic

Frénaud

Bonnefoy

Roche

Pleynet

"So, nu! HOW about some women POETS?"

When they reached Boulevard Haussmann, they stopped in front of 102 : "Check out the  first floor for Marcel Proust. Further up, a married lady to whom he wrote touching letters, often carried to her by her dentist husband." She was a harpist like Harpo Marx.

SKINNY: "Watch your language!"

FATSO: "Are you alluding to…"
SKINNY: "                                             "

In the bedroom, there was a button you could push so that the curtains would close.

As of that first night, if she hadn't junked it from her memory, she had become a love object, obviously by  a Chair deprived.

She found a degree of consolation, looking at her image in the ceiling mirror.

Mirrors reminded her of table 38.

She said to herself: "Stop thinking. It's bad for your health." She wondered, as she tried to fall back to sleep, if what she was doing might not be a masterpiece of philosophy, maybe taken out of Bergson?"

As we waited, at our dining table, when the food hadn't yet arrived, a waiter came over to each table, and filled our champagne glasses with champagne.

The food hadn't yet come over to our elegant table.

More champagne from Champagne.

I tried, but I couldn't get my father's face out of my eyes.

She remembered how difficult it was to get his garden boots off, when he had had too much to drink! Then, he'd retell us, for the endless time, what it was like, in the war, and how he had killed some Armenian, with that rifle above the fireplace.

He farted.

I asked my mother how she could live through those memories, and how she would have wanted to break each bottle of wine they kept on the shelf.

All of a sudden, and for no apparent reason, a red convertible waited for me outside. A red MG, taking me to church.

Might it have been tourists thrown out of that car by wandering bandits?

Somebody wanted to give me driving lessons.

Always suspicious, my mother intervened, and said, in an affirmative voice: "Leave my daughter alone, you prospective rapist!"

I escaped, even though I would really have wanted to go for a ride!

My mother took me back inside, and taught me how to sew a hem. She taught me how to grill a pig's feet and many other things!

I remembered all of that, as I stepped out of that elegant hotel bathroom, drying myself with one of those huge, thick, immaculate yellow towels. I knew they'd be taken away by a maid, and machine-washed in the cellar.

He woke up, out of a deep slumber, and asked me, after we had seen a Durer exhibit, whether Durer had only painted a hum-drum Eve, giving Adam an apple, or, might it have been, for a second, Adam sliding a pomegranate into Eve's mouth? Then the whole of Christianity might have been forced to revise its teachings on small paintings and on church walls!

Ave Maria! Or Eve!

He wondered if his parents would denounce him to the PAPAL Police?

(Could he have been the "Fourth Tempter," in T.S. Eliot's "Murder in the Cathedral"?)

(She wished, in despair, that, if all the water in the pool had seeped out, leaving the empty pool. until a group of high-flying millionaires decided to fill 'er up once more!

 How different her life might have been, in a real pool!

In her repetitive dream, her father washed his hands of all that blood in battle.

How the past shadowed the present!

She slipped off her bike. Hurt her left thumb.

Would someone make a quick call to our village ambulance?

She got back on, and biked to the Indiscreet Jewel.

Danced.  Kissed.  Body-to-Body. Tourists glared at us. Some asked our permission to take a picture of us.

I said yes, since I always carried my Leica with me, in my handbag. I, too, have taken oodles of pictures in the Indiscreet, developed them all, and pinned them up in my dark room.

A note: "I'll see you back at the university!"

She dyed her hair blond, to escape her identity.

(Dreams squeezed in, floated  by, searching for a quick identity trick.)

She bleached her eyebrows.

She painted her fingernails in bright pink.

When night came to a close, I threw the sheets to the side, looked at my vagina, and decided to paint it blue.

The Chair couldn't recognize me!

A G.I. jeep stopped.

Saw me drenched.

Asked if he could drive me to his place. He said he had so many army things,  he could easily give me a couple of shirts to get me dressed again! He admired my Leica.

"I love your telephoto lenses!"

ENTER

QUOTE: "You'll never guess it!"

FATSO: "Haven't I read all those words before?"

SKINNY: "Repetition is our way of being!"

She faked her answer, saying she had found it in the garbage of her house, destroyed.  Later, she told me the truth, or was it ever the truth, that that Leica had belonged to her father."My father said he had bought it in Poland, immediately after the war." Later, he found out they kept the body with slight changes, so that US troops would buy it.

The captain took a whiff of the truth and, turning around, after having checked my lenses, said he, too, had a camera that had been given to him on his sixth birthday by his aunt.

"Take what you need."

Then he added, I should take anything else that seemed to me to be interesting.

 FATSO: "Must all novels be autobiographical?"

SKINNY: "All novels ARE autobio. of all preceding novels! WHEN YOU WRITE, YOU BOTH admire other novels or wish they had never existed. As for literature…the same! Why do you ask so many questions?"

FATSO: "The only thing left for me, at this moment, is to continue clicking questions, until the end. In fact, I saw reality through my images."

BESIDES, BOTH SAID, SIMULTANEOUSLY: "You can substitute one thing for another! Besides

(…) you know what I mean?"

The young, militarily dressed Turkish friend, a recently appointed friend, said: "G.I., have you ever fucked a Turk?"

In the emptiness of sounds, he answered silently:

"No! You're the first one to ask! In my time, people couldn't have found a Turkish woman, except as a cleaning woman, or as a highly selected baby sitter! "

Did she have a dark room, somewhere on this deserted block? Her Leica…She had bartered her aunt's necklace for film.  My Turkish lady photographer said images are footprints on a sandy beach! How she would have wanted to take pictures in the bus, pictures of people and their countryside!"

I still had an image of my father, pushing me on a make-shift swing in the back yard!

I still had an image of Cossacks, firing on my three girlfriends, one with a crying baby carriage down Odessa steps! How I wish I had had my Leica, at that moment, or a movie camera!

Why did mother always stay in the kitchen? Where were my older brothers? Did they leave our country, to go somewhere else, to study accounting or … She listened to two overweight friends.

FATSO : "I warned you, Berlin doesn't really exist, at all! It's all in somebody's mind!"

SKINNY: "Are you delusional?"

She told them where to stand, in front of a partially existing wall. "There!! A souvenir shot!"

Leica positioned herself, and snapped pictures of FATSO AND SKINNY, against a crumbling wall, actually, but, as she remembered it, with a ready vomit, not far from the pool.

Then she said: "You're right! Berlin is a shell of its forgotten languages, except for stairs leading to another Jew."

Captain says: "Stop—all those forgotten walls!"

THE END OR IS IT?

(So ends this peregrination.)

Xxxxxxxxxxxxxxxxxxxxxxxxxxxxxxxxxxxxxxxxxxxxxxxxxxxxxxxxxxxxxxxxxxxxx

P.S

12. Keep right to stay on 1-81 N, follow signs for 1.-88/Syracuse/Albany

13. Take the exit onto 1-690 W toward Fairgrounds/Baldwinsville

14. Take exit 2 for Jones Rd.

# THE TRUTH
## IS THE FAMILY

NEW YORK

y mother

Reads the lst canons of the Old Testament. Our next door-neighbor yells out: "Next year in the Bronx!"

The Torah, and within it, Genesis, Exodus, Leviticus, Numbers, Deuteronomy.

My father reminded us, around the kitchen table....

That we had

Nowhere else to sit down,

So we called our Kitchen Our Living Room.

Mother stopped my Father.

She looked around, at all of us, and smiled. She hoped one more son would become a rabbi, and Another One, the boy with a beautiful voice, whom we heard singing in the shower. (Mother Remembered, and…
We never forgot it.)  In the old days, showers were taken in the kitchen, in a large brown tub, filled with luke warm water, poured on us, to wash our hair. There, he sang.

"A future cantor," She said.

In the Torah, the first family mentioned, was a family, and she said, the history of the Jewish
People

Began with the history of the family.

Mother stopped.

She looked around our small dinner table, and she was sure our family must have been like
the very first One. We went to synagogue, around the corner, on Holy Days, when the men
wore sneakers. She also Knew the larger portion of a heritage (if ever we could get to that!)
would go to the Oldest Boy. That Was Me!

Every year, she would say:

"Our family follows the Torah."

Out of our building, next to poverty, we walked to synagogue, around the corner. No one can

Forget the Sabbath!

She had been told by her father, of members of a Jewish sect (the word horrified me!)
mourning over

The Destruction of the Temple.

Father interrupted, and said how he would have wanted to belong to an

Ascetic movement among the Karaites in Jerusalem.

Mother would add her own translation of the
Haggadah, which included the Everything in Talmudic Literature.

She looked at me.

I said, in a serious voice, that the Love of God had already been described by Maimonides.

Then the meal.

(Better than Hebrew National! Even with Gulden mustard)

(It took a long time to discover what father did when he said he worked off 5th Avenue, in the diamond District.)

But we learned (how?) he was paid a miserly salary, as a broom sweeper, after closing hours. He loved a Glass of Manischewitz . After a glass, he drank one more glass, until his head was Ready to slump down, on the kitchen table. At that instant, mother would tickle his neck, and he would Jump Up, slowly.

But, then again, he started talking about his death and, looking at me, the eldest son, he would say: "You won't inherit a thing!"

 Mother added "The life we lead is a hem! Perhaps all of what we did was to live through clothing! We sweep away the cobwebs of our past, as quickly as possible!"


Mother cleaned out the bedroom, to get rid of the stink.

Somebody, next to her, recited a line of poetry: ...

"...and I've been to all the graves."

I wondered if mother had ever seen a film by Buñuel?

Fils added: "Did Papa ever mention French anti-semitism?"

Maman answered: "When you grow up, you should read Sartre's "Réflexions sur la question juive," where he

Says, anti-semitism is equal to anti- Chinese, anti- Blacks, anti- North Africans,

Especially Berbers, who all speak French! All of them are part of a

Bourgeois Collective Hate. A real passion."

Then, Sartre added,

"All of them are part of a small town bourgeoisie "

Then, he noted that all Frenchmen believe France belonged to them. Did he know all about Nazis

Executions of Jews?

'Of children?

Of old grand-parents?"

Then, she added: "if you really want more info, read  Serge Klarsfeld, who carries their memory, for

Instance, and the dates of all the trains, taking them to Poland—all trains run by French engineers.  He

Knew

That

148

Karol Pila, 12 yrs old, died in Auschwitz-Birkenau.

He knew the number of all extermination trains.

He knew the President of the United States

Refused to bomb the tracks, leading to THE death camp.

Maman knew that her niece, during the early years of the war, took her three daughters out of

Paris, to

A hole to

Hide them in a small mountain

Village,

Where her three daughters were baptized.

They were also told to hide their noses, when they went out.

When the war was over, the girls were told they were Jewish.

"That's impossible," they chorused:

"We went to church every Sunday, and prayed, and sang!"

(You couldn't change their minds.)

Fils knew maman was an adamant ordained Francophile, but, with an effort, she did become

an ardent

Jewish mother!

She loved gefilte fish from Zabar, picked up, on the right, on the second shelf, when

You walked into the store.

(It could have been Murray's or Barney Greengrass. But she truly loved Café Edison, for their very

Great pastrami and borscht.)

She also bought Rose's horseradish, red or white!

Once in a while, with her best friend, she'd succumb to a salami sandwich at Katz's.

How many other goodies, she said, in

A whisper, could she find…

LET'S SAY

Israeli-made matzos, tongue for holidays, salmon, and all sorts of

Veggies, and, after dinner, ice-cream and cookies and teas, in multiple organic bags…

(Prayers,

All the time!)

Maman said: "When the war's over, you'll take the

"France,"

"The jewel of the French Line" and go, as quickly

As possible, visit your grand-mother, in Marseilles. No use telling her not to prepare a pastry feast for

You!

"You'll stay in Katia's apartment.

"If you pull out the center drawer, of that chest

 Of drawers, in your bedroom, you'll get a whiff of a very

Old perfume, and you'll see a scratched-up crystal flask. And, next to it, a revolver, wrapped

up in an old

Towel.

That morning, you'll ask Génia about that gun!

He won't answer.

His wife, your aunt, tells you he never talks about his patriotic actions, in the Massif Central,

where he

Caught British guns, FROM THE SKY, dropped off, by the British, for our Resistance. He gave

them out to

His fighting men.

Génia never spoke about his Resistance activities. He did say, one day, one of his men told

Him that, if they didn't act to save the men, below, lined up in the village square, all of them

rounded up,

They'd all be shot against the Church wall.

"We should go down and save them!"

René Char answered: "If we do, there's a chance we'll all be killed, and our Resistance would come to a bloody

End."

He asked us, if we knew that, after the war, in Kai-Fong-fou, a handful of Chinese didn't eat pork.

Génia also told me about Jews in India, and then in Greece.

"Is your Unk. a historian?" asked my friend.

He told us about the founding of Alexandria, about three centuries, before Christ. Then he mentioned

Caligula and Claudius. ("Who the hell are they?")

He told us about a terrible pogrom in the 30th year of our time.

"Stop!" She said. "Enough is enough!"

Under his breath, he added: "Did we know all Jews were always fucked over, wherever they lived?"

I knew Maman wanted to perfect her knowledge of American lit.to perfect her new tongue!

She spoke of

"Moby Dick."

She added that, in Genesis, 21,

"God created great whales."

Then, she told us that, in Deuteronomy, Moses said God had not forgotten captains, and he created

Thousands of them!

We heard that Ishmael was the son of Agar.

We all knew God had written Genesis, all by himself!

She quoted a passage from:

"Moby Dick."

"Sweet fields beyond the swelling flood, stand dressed in living green."

(Words words words words, and .others)

We knew she always looked for French words in all novels.

Like:

Bourbons

Tuilleries

Fils changed the topic, turned to his father's place, in bed:

"On papa's side, I saw a fat copy of "War

And Peace."

Maman says: "You're too young to check out Napoleon's troops!"

She added: "Probably, you can't even spell the author's name! Remember, your papa was born

in tsarist


Russia!


For him, Tolstoy is a house-hold name!


In the present tense!"


"I know that!"


"Don't interrupt!"


"Ok!"


Maman says to me:


"Have you ever heard of Prince Nesvitski?


Probably not!"


"Have you ever heard the word "bourgeois?"


"Your papa comes from that easy class, with servants, a


Horses and a carriage."


He remembers that, as a young man,


His parents ate caviar with a soup spoon! He


Must have told you his father was a well-known dentist.

Because of him, he saw a rehearsal of a play by

Checkoff (✓)

He saw a great ballerina dance! He heard play a famous French pianist.

Now, at 15 West 107th street, on the fifth floor. When you walk down our corridor, to the

right, you'll

See

Your father's room and, in it, a dentist's drill!  He

Couldn't legally practice, in the US, but he did drill, on the side!

He fixed lots of Russian teeth!"

"But, why "War and Peace?"


"Your father believes Tolstoy is a far greater writer than: "Crime and Punishment."
For

Your father, that author is not a fine writer! Your father says, a good beginning doesn't work, if
you're

Not a great writer!"

Fils: "Is there a character papa loves best?"

Maman answers: "Tolstoy says it best, in Book Ten, chapter 6, where he writes:" Matter and

form."

"That's it, in a Russian nut shell! Or, if you prefer, a Russian Easter egg!"

"Then, when he really wanted to impress his public…"

Maman sliced in a new list of English literary expressions she picked up in a Zane Grey

Novel:

 "I thought and thought, despite the

darknessafraidofthedarkness darkened mercifully Bloody blot

                                        Sickening nausea

 Concluded his narrative."

                                        "Now…"

Now, all of us had heard snatches of that list, slip into her vocabulary…

"And, maman, what about your father?"

Maman: "Oy! What a life HE Led!"

"I'll read you a couple of pages of his Memoir, and you'll see what kind of a life he lived, in

Siberia! I'll

Give you his "Memoir of a Soldier of the Revolution!" It's easy to read! It'll only take you a

couple of

Hours!"

Maman added: "Here's a couple of lines, from his life, as a prisoner in the salt mines…"

She paused

And, a minute later, she was about to read:

FROM HIS WRITING

Fils: "That's enough to fill up lots, and lots of pages! When I finish my homework, I'll read it! "

"By the way, anything else about Tolstoy, I should know?"

Maman:"Well, one of your father's weirdest interests was to check out French passages in

Tolstoy! He

Actually believes that our family's name might be related to count Vronski, in "Anna Karenina."

What a

Love story! What a scene at the RR station!"

"Sometimes (maman, added) and both in France and in America, Feminism seems to have

sprung up, in

A now

Fashionable manner! But, all you have to do, is read Tolstoy's views on women, and…forget,

for the

Moment,

American feminist ideology, when Lilith comes riding in!"

Tolstoy writes, about society women: Here's the quote:

"Selfish, vain, stupid, trivial in everything."

"…well, your papa was clear about the following, as he changed radically from what we were talking

About to…"

He said: "if we had stayed in St. Petersburg, or later on, in Paris, Pétain would have turned all of us in!

And, all that, with a simple phone call from Vichy."

"By the way, two little things worth noting: first: all the French who do not feel perfect in their

stomachs, go to Vichy, for the bath or something like that, and paid for by Social Security. They walk around

With tin cups!

Could it be THEIR urine?

The other thing they say about Pétain: "He loved  feeling up

handmaids' assesses, in his hotel staircases!"

 Otherwise, for children, there's a beautiful playground, with lots of colors.

Otherwise, he'd turn all of us over to Paris Gendarmes. Don't they look Great, these elegant Nazis, having

To ask someone to

Take their pictures, in front of the "Arc de Triomphe! With a long-lensed-Leica.

Then, he added: "If we had stayed in our apartment, on rue Sévero, soon enough, we'd all be wearing

The Yellow Star on our left lapels."

I heard maman and papa speak in their foreign tongue!

When I asked, they'd say:

In a heavy Russian accent,

"Russian."

October 3, 1940, all Jews had to show up at their Police Station. The one closest to where they

Lived.

In our case, the Police Station, on Avenue du Maine.

(Not far from an expensive fish restaurant!)

Maman told me, we were fantastically lucky! She added:

"We went from Paris to the South, where a dear friend of your father's, had a small house, made for

Farm

Tools.

He said, if we didn't make too much noise, we could stay there, for a longish time! He saved our

Lives, at least for a longish moment!"

To make ourselves useful, all of us, holding wicker baskets, went picking grapes in his vines.

I ate so many grapes I got nightlong diarrheas!"

"And you? What ever happened to you?"

"My parents were still in the so-called Unoccupied France! You know, a while later, the whole of France

Was occupied.

They say, in the summer of '42, the Paris police rounded up all Jews, living in Paris. At least those whom

they could find.

I escaped.

I didn't look Jewish.

"Maman, can papa read English? I'm asking because Tolstoy, in his "Circle of Reading," must have

Read Thoreau and Emerson! I heard that, both of them, were greatly admired in the 19th century! All

those pages on Papa's side of the bed!"

"You just mentioned our New York apartment, our now

Apartment, off Broadway!"

"How's your memory? "

"I mean, what do you remember best about our fourth floor apartment?"

Maman answers her own question:

"Of course,

You must remember!

Cockroaches, all along the kitchen

floor! Your papa

Bought some white stuff,

And lined the kitchen floor with it! He was sure that would stop that invasion,

of all those black beasties! At least, for a time being!"

Fils: "Maman, did I tell you, in my trolley car, I started talking to somebody, who must have

been my a

Age,

I told him how I got into Bentley School, 48 West 86th Street, between Central Park West and

Columbus Avenue.

I told him the school needed a French accent.

 Also, and I've got to tell you this, when the biology professor was doing his thing on

color blindness, I was always called in!

All the girls would ask me: "What's the color of my cashmere sweater?"

I was like

Salad dressing, in that private school.

The Principal, Mrs. Kaufman, wrote letters of recommendations for all our college

Applications! She watched us, very carefully, so that the letter would be both academic and

personal! I

told you, we were like clichés, us poor immigrants! All the girls wore colorful cashmere

sweaters, and

Florida suntans! I fell in love, at first sight, with Elaine! She lived in what was then called an

Art Nouveau

Building. on West End Avenue. When they had a party, at her home, her parents stayed with

us, to

Make

Sure we wouldn't ravage their liquor closet!

After graduation, I so wanted to see her again, and not at one

Of our school dances, when we cleared out the assembly hall, and pushed chairs to the side!

How, once a year, we'd put on a show.

That year: "Ballad for Americans."

We listened to Paul Robeson

His thing with that musical.

And then we tried to imitate!

I pinched Elaine in the staircase.

I felt rejected, on the 2nd floor, when she pushed my lips aside. I had

hoped she'd love me because…she didn't turn me in! I ran up to the fourth floor, still hoping

she

Wouldn't reject me.

"Me: me, with that unloved tongue! "

 We rehearsed:

"Ballad…"

I couldn't stop dreaming my ferocious hand would do its work!

I'd kiss her innocent breasts.

Her barely

ripe nipples.

My real, only friend, in High School, was Shmuel Shwartz. Together, we'd go down to Town

Hall, and listen to

Great

Political debates!

By now, he's a big-time lawyer, probably living on Park Avenue, near that church, in the nineties! I think, by now, he must have a house, somewhere in Sag Harbor, next to a

Potato farm!"

Maman:"In a couple of years, when you continue doing the right things in class, you'll' go to college!

God, I hope you'll stay in New York! I'm still hoping you won't be drafted, and sent to Korea…"

Fils: "I asked maman to ask that question to a fortune teller, on Houston, not far from that giant movie

House!"

In the meantime, a college buddy of mine said that, if I really didn't want to go to Korea, all I had to do

Was to say that, the very first sergeant I'd see, I'd knife him!

I was sent to see a psychiatrist.

He: «Vat dou u dink habut ur parents?»

I answered:

"Somtimes yes, sometimes, no!»

He asked:

"Vat ubut goils?"

I answered :

”Sometimes yes, sometimes, no!”

A little later,

A doctor slipped his finger up my ass, to make sure, when I was drafted, that I had no diseases.

Then…

The doctor twiddled my balls.

He asked:

”Do u vish me 2 go on?”

I answered:

”Yes, why not!”

He wrote down, on a brown piece of army paper:

“Highly aggressiff, gut four di armiy!”

Then, in Fort Dix, my hair shaved off, I was ordered to the orderly room.

The captain, standing upright, asked a group of us:

“if we still wanted to be considered a bunch of nuts?  If so, look for 18 months of peeling

potatoes!”

“Those of you who have changed your minds, step forward!”

All, 15 of us, stepped forward.

I told mother, we first went to Seattle, and then, by ship, to Korea.

A longish trip.

We anchored in Pusan, and then, in trucks, driven to Seoul.

There, I took pictures, with that old camera you gave

me!

Pictures of bullet- holed walls, on downtown buildings.

Maman:"I hope, after your graduation, you'll be like Tiresias! Words in the future.

Who will I be in the

Near future? '

"Besides, I know, by now, you've switched from Sartre to Lacan, or was it Barthes'

"Semiology"?

Fils: Later on I knew, my mother's dear friend, Mrs. Gold-

Stone, was a

Seamstress on the Lower East Side! She had a son who changed his name to Bernie.

Is

always an "is"?

Or, maybe, he'd become a "Yesterday"?

I mean, I heard from my Ph.D English high school professor say, how Lacan questioned

Foucault's

166

Epistemology!

Then, at school breaks, the teach said, (actually, there were no breaks!)

smiling, two

Names, nobody recognized: Baudrillard and Lyotard.

Then, he wished how he hoped Lacan would be pissed off when Freud

Didn't name him, his own rep. in Paris!

Lacan, they say, called Marie Bonaparte, Freud's choice, or was that Derrida's term?

"The cook in the kitchen," even if she was to

Write a psychoanalytical interpretation of Edgar Poe, with a preface by Freud! And, a picture

of Poe,

Smack on the cover!

Then, the Hungarian fencing coach continued, by saying, in his foreign accent:" if we wanted

clarity, we

Should all read Saussure and Paul de Man, and his linguistic approach to reading a literary

text, like

Rousseau's "Confessions."

We should all say:

"To hell with History or Biographies! Only lust for the naked Truth!"

He was so proud of being a Russian formalist! He knew he had us by the balls!

I heard maman whisper, something like:

"You can't do all of that! That's all petty bourgeois! says a Marxism

Refridgerated!"

Papa read the "Forward," in Yiddish.

He said he really wanted to have one of those Zane Grey Texas Rangers'

English.

Actually, nothing moved him-- when he smiled-- when we rehearsed  "Ballad for Americans!"

I heard mommy (her naturalized American name) shake papa, during the night.

She would say: "Shatzy,

What are you dreaming about?"

He answered:

"Mommy, I remember how I passed my grammar test in Bangladeshi! You know, my dream

was always

To represent the down-trodden, like those Carmel drivers, in their

Carmel limos."

She said to papa: "I remember when we got married, by a rabbi in St. Petersburg! You were so

Handsome!"

He said:

168

"You, too!"

Then, he added: "Marxism is exploding! Now, PACS, when queers, in France, die, the other one

inherits their boyfriend's

Apartment, and all the money in the bank, in his name, at least! "

She said: "Just read my father's "Memoirs."

"Remember, how Abraham saved us, with his money in Lisbon, and then, he continued, once we got to

New York!"

Bernie: "You smell garlic!"

So he gave it a thought!

Papa walked through Central Park.

He saw Abraham, checking his bank account, in a Madison Avenue bank, near an art gallery.

(Then I heard father, once back in the kitchen, where he thought he had killed off all those roaches!...

I

Heard him piss. )

(He always closed the door, so we wouldn't hear him! Sometimes, he opened the faucet

And let water drip down.)

He said, in Russian, confidentially: "I'm a urine factory!"

A holiday came, every Saturday.

Mommy would say: "we'll all have salmon, on whole wheat bagels, with cream cheese, a slice

Of a beef steak tomato, and, a king size round of onion!"

She'd say:

She'd say, she had

Piles and piles of black and green olives

She'd picked up at Zabar's, right on the left, when you walked in and, before all those Long

Island

Ladies stormed in out of their bus!"

Number 22: "That's me!" She pointed to a huge white fish: That one, please."

"Hazel, you're nuts! What are you going to do with all of that?"

And she added: "What about you, staring at that three level of goodies? I saw you throwing in

a paper

Cup

Potato salad. In another one, creamed herring. I can't even name all of the others! Who's going

to eat

All of

That?"

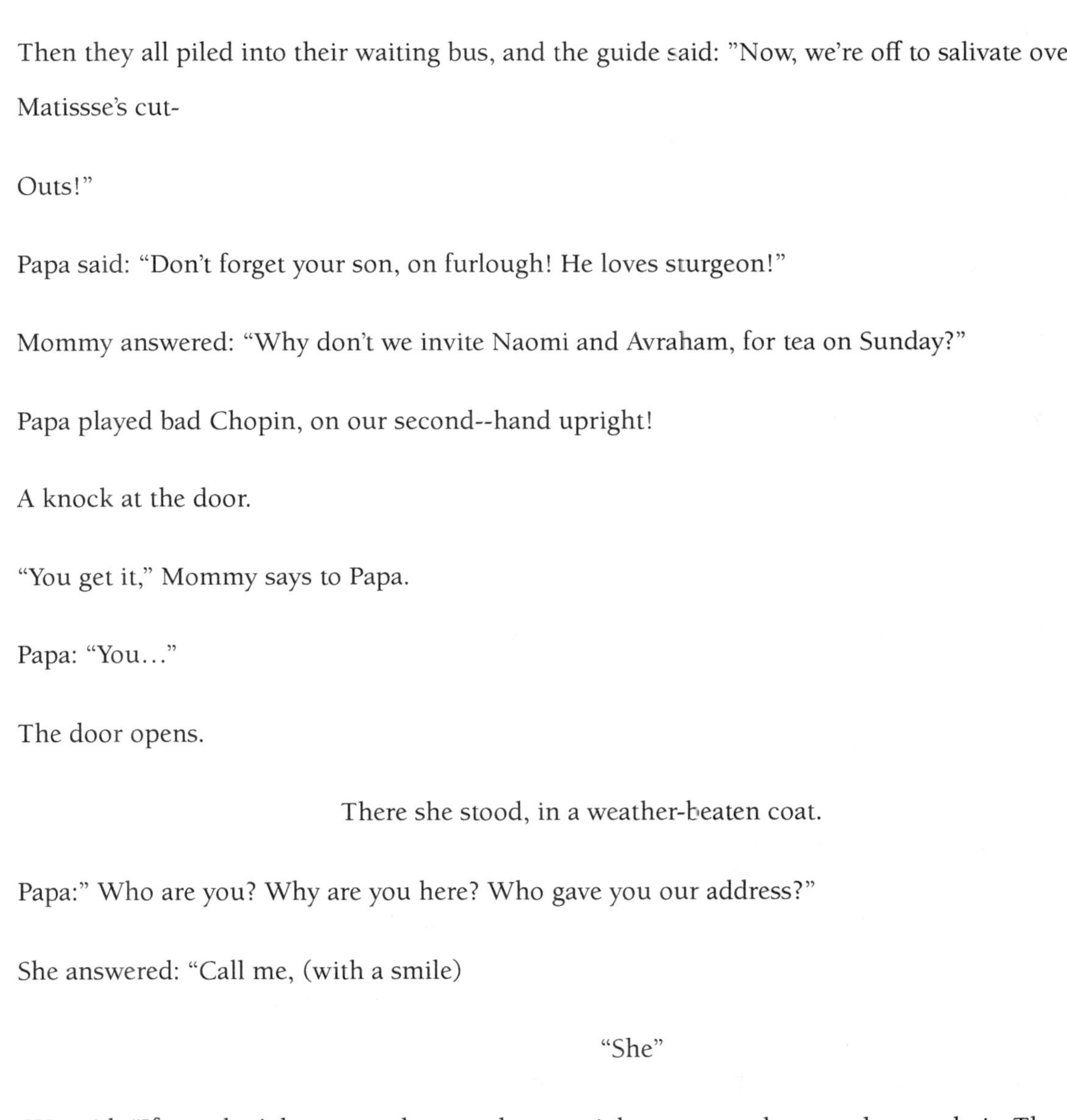

"In the freezer!"

Then they all piled into their waiting bus, and the guide said: "Now, we're off to salivate over Matissse's cut-

Outs!"

Papa said: "Don't forget your son, on furlough! He loves sturgeon!"

Mommy answered: "Why don't we invite Naomi and Avraham, for tea on Sunday?"

Papa played bad Chopin, on our second--hand upright!

A knock at the door.

"You get it," Mommy says to Papa.

Papa: "You…"

The door opens.

There she stood, in a weather-beaten coat.

Papa:" Who are you? Why are you here? Who gave you our address?"

She answered: "Call me, (with a smile)

"She"

 We said: "If you don't have anywhere to sleep, tonight, you can sleep on the couch, in The living room…"

Then "She" added:

"Madame Noir, in Paris, she  knows you. She still lives at 107 bld de Montparnasse. She said to me, her

Family….

Knew your family in St. Petersburg!

She changed her name, to Noir, when she settled in Paris.

Rather than coming to the States as Noir, she came up with Schwartz,

Instead of Noir! Then she became black and then Blake."

"By the way, I wonder whatever happened to that couple, that white Rolls Royce, left in front of our bus,

When the door closed? I think I've seen that RR on Georgica Lane. They can wait on the bench, under

One

Of our gorgeous linden trees and wait for the next one, around 3 o'clock!"

Mommy: "May I interrupt? Please, at night, when we let you sleep on the couch in

The living room, please don't flush, as you might like to do, three times a night!"

Papa: "Let's believe, for a moment, she's our distant daughter, come back!"

She: "The first time, when I tried to remember what Mrs Noir said about what she thought your dining

Room looked like, from what her friends had told her, I know I'll make a mistake and come through

The swinging kitchen door,

Leading to the dining room, and that large table!

"Let me ask you, I saw two pictures above that old upright, of two people.

Who they are?"

"The first, is my father. The empty frame next to him is my grandfather: I couldn't get a

picture of my

Grandfather!"

Mommy: "The boy's no longer a boy! He finished Columbia College, with a BA, with honors in

 European

History, then he went on to graduate school and, he was barely finished, when he was drafted!
Now,

He's in

Korea! BUT, here's another one: When he was 5 yrs old, in Leningrad, he loved to fold paper

Planes. He loved to launch them over the Neva. He applauded, when they flew. He broke into a

huge

Laughter, when they landed on the Neva! Then, when they sank, he'd flip! ONLY OLD Soviet

fighter

Planes could see them, floating beneath the surface! If you want my truth,

*And, I 'd see the Nile! I'd see my little boy's planes, flying over the Nile, and, maybe, find out from*

*where I*

*Might*

*Have come from!"*

                    *I, well,*                             *OOPS!*

*(words words…)*


*You know, we Russian Jews, in exile…well, we're really all Puritans! One*

*Day, our son said: 'Damn,' and papa slapped him right on the kisser: Isn't that an American woid?*
*Also,*

*And, this a secret, and never say anything about what I'm going to tell you, promise? When he was*

*About*

*12, I snuck into his room, to make his bed. I pulled the sheets towards me and, I saw a piece of*

*paper*

*Beneath his bed! It had lots of names on it, and all of them in a single column. Here it is:*

Dr. Zismore

Moses

Tuff Kentridge

Daddy Day's

Care Mary

Curry Bonne

Mommy says:"

Go!

All you gangsters

Faux pas (Don't do it!)

Groin grow up

"Oy!"

Sister

Shafty quizzy

Me

"That's my father's picture!"

Bernie: "Who's the old man with a beard, and glasses, you keep above the piano?"

Mommy says: "Here goes, with my father's memoirs:

When he was in Siberia, slaving away in a salt mine,

This is what he wrote:

"Did you bring the drills from the forge? I was far, far away, in Russia…So, this was hard

labor? Day after

Day, I climbed the mountain, and banged the granite, like a madman. In the pit, I stood there,

blinking,

Perplexed.  Little by little, my eyes got used to the dark. You see, you've got to dig out the

stone… By the

Way, see this overhead? You better hope it doesn't come down! Then the food: for  meat…

intestines,

Lips,

Ears,

Tails,

And other pieces.

"Hunger, as the Russian say, is not your aunt."  Always careful to hold your Hand

Steady, so that you don't hit your thumb, and, in fact, once I rested, I managed to drill with

better

Results. Hadn't I been condemned to hard labor: "In perpetuity?"

Bernie: "Ok! Ok! I got it!"

Mommy: "I forget to tell you: when I found that unexpected list, I also found a question of his past! You

Asked, to whom did that portrait belong? I saw, written on a piece of paper, right after that picture.

Bernie: "What did it say?"

**MINOR, SOLOMON ZALMAN** (Zalkind; 1826–1900), writer and scholar, one of the pioneers of the Russian-Jewish intelligentsia. As a youth, he entered the newly opened government rabbinical seminary in Vilna and was one of its first two graduates—he was later a Talmud teacher in his seminary. Through the efforts of the *maskilim* he was elected *kazyonny ravvin* ("government-appointed rabbi") of the Minsk community in 1859. One of the first to preach in Russian in the synagogue, he became well known for his sermons, which were published in book form and served as models for other rabbis. Minor was active in the promotion of *Haskalah in Minsk, and in 1869 he was invited to serve as rabbi in Moscow. In the early 1890s, when the Jews of Moscow were persecuted, he interceded with the authorities on behalf of his community and was consequently expelled from Moscow on the order of the governor of the city, the Grand Duke Sergei. He then returned to Vilna and continued his literary activity there. Minor published many articles in the Russian-Jewish and the Hebrew press, for the most part under the name "Remez." He conducted a debate with anti-Semites (including the priest *Lutostansky) and was a friend of Tolstoy and directed his studies in Hebrew and the Bible. He was one of the first Jewish scholars to work in the field of the history of Russian Jewry. His son LAZAR (ELIEZER) MINOR was a professor of nervous diseases and another son, Osip *Minor, was a leader of the Social Revolutionary Party.

**Bibliography:** J. Slutsky in: *He-Avar,* 7 (1960), 29–48; S. Guenzburg, in: *Knizhki Voskhoda,* 2 (1901), 128–35; A. Katzenelson. in: *Yevrevskaya Starina* 2 (1909) 175–88 [Y.S.]

**MINOR, OSIP S.** (Joseph; 1861–1932), Russian revolutionary and a leader of the Social Revolutionary Party. Born in Minsk, he was the son of Rabbi S. Z. *Minor. While still a student at the University of Moscow, he joined the "People's Will" (Narodnaya Volya) Society. In 1883 he was arrested for the first time, and in 1887 he was exiled to Siberia. After participating in a rebellion of exiles in Yakutsk, he was sentenced to forced labor for life (1889). Freed in 1896, he was banned from living in European Russia. In 1900 he nevertheless returned to Russia and settled in Vilna. He resumed his revolutionary activities, traveled abroad, and was one of the organizers of the Social Revolutionary Party. In 1909 he was again arrested as a result of the intervention of the czarist agent Y. F. *Azeff and was sentenced to ten years' forced labor. He was freed at the time of the Revolution of 1917 and was briefly mayor of Moscow. Minor left Russia in 1919 after the Bolshevik victory and settled in France, where he became chairman of the Society for Assistance to Exiles and Political Prisoners in Russia. He died in Paris. His book *Eto bylo davno* ("It Was Long Ago") appeared posthumously in 1933.

**Bibliography:** *Sotsialisticheskiy Vestnik,* 19 (1932), 16; V. Chernov, *Yidishe Tuer in der Partey Sotsial Revolutsionern* (1948), 246–58.　　　　　　　　　　　　　　　　　　　　[Y.S.]

And here's my great grandfather's entry in that same Encyclopedia. Just like the one i promised you!"

"Now, for that empty frame: I found him out elsewhere!"

She: "And the girl?"

Mommy: "Another time."

Bernie: "How about right now?"

Mommy: "So, I began reading my father's memoirs, about his memory of Siberia!"

poet

poet

poet

poet

poet

…and others words.

Papa (whispered)" Why not make her our moment's daughter?"

She: (Checks out our Bible and reads a page.)

"I know the wall was destroyed."

She added:

"I feel like mosaics torn apart by the Romans! Temple walls turned upside down."

Papa: "Where did you get all that?"

Mommy:"She'll say, she's part of the past present! Then, I'll tell her once more, don't flush in the

Middle of the night! I know that, from your father's visits! He says he's a urine factory!  Later, I can add

Some

Food.

I remember eating half a buttered baguette, some strawberry jam, on the side, and there, I

Was, drinking my morning coffee, at a bar on Ave du Maine, corner rue des Plantes.  If I close my

Eyes, I see myself

Walking past that

Huge, Ugly Lion de Belfort statue!

I can still feel my legs ache, when I walk down those métro steps!"

Papa :"You make me sick with your eternal memory!"

Mommy: "It's one of my only real pleasures left! What about yours? Don't tell me you've forgotten

Tolstoy? Myself, I close my ears in the subway. it's now, an old Parisian habit!  And there, I hear plans for a

Summer

Vacation, and they're already trying to compare

Their last vacation's meals, with what they dream about, for the next one! That afternoon, in a bus near

Pompidou, a kid's crying.

Half the bus turns around

And, in a chorus. say:

"Manners! Teach that yelling

Kid some manners!"

She remembers how her father gave her a real slap, on the left cheek, when she

Had her hands under the table.

And he said:

"What are you doing, down there?"

That's when I learned

Lots of things and, for example, when my father slapped me! Then, when the bus stopped, a

thousand

Passengers ran to the center door, as others tried to get in! When I waited for the next bus, I

couldn't

Forget those huge publicity posters, on all métro walls!  I read about a concert, vacations in

Tunisia, a sale Au Bon Marché, and six huge rolls of toilet paper, with a baby seating on top!"

Papa : "Can't you stop living elsewhere?  You sound like a recent arrival in Paris, from St.

Petersburg!

And why do you keep that wrinkled letter, written in Russian? "

Mommy:"Why don't you ask our new guest to put her suitcase down! Now, she's reading

René Magritte: "Ecrits

complets » (Paris:Textes-Flammarion, 1979)

«Un homme du peuple, sans douter de la mort de sa femme… » (p. 316)

When she unpacked, a book slipped out: Geoffrey Hartman's:"Saving the Text."

On our out- of- tune upright, she played Chopin, or was it Schubert? For me, in her heavy

Russian

Accent, she's a

Talking postcard from St. Petersburg! "

Now, she's crying! I say to her: "We're not in "Russian" anymore!"

I told you a little bit about my father, and his biography. You can find him in the Jewish

Encyclopedia.

"Here goes!"

Son:

"My mother's Grandfather must have been a big deal rabbi! That's what happens to sons of the

bourgeoisie:

Revolutionaries!"

Velodia, my son's friend, said: "Many thanks for that info. !'d like to give you very precise info on your great-grandfather…

Mommy:"Dear son, after Velodia, read everything, don't you think you've got a pound of socialism in

You, and an equal part of religion? By the way, I want to thank you for all those beautiful postcards you

Sent, when you traveled all over the Far East!! Wherever you traveled to, once a week, a postcard! I

Look inside that wooden box, and you'll see all of your post-cards! I opened this box again and again, and

I read

The back of all the Pictures! Have you got anything else, from a micro-revolutionary point of view?"

Jonathan: "I saved the Army's morale! And, I didn't do it, during my R&R!"

Mommy: "How?"

Jonathan: "Here I am, finishing my day's duty,  as part of  8th U.S. Army, stationed in Seoul. My captain

Says, in a half-whisper

To all of us:

"Gonnorhea."

("OK! I say to myself! No cunts today!")

Mommy:"Save me from your Army Lingo!"

Jonathan:"I'm walking down the DMZ. For you, the Demilitorized Zone, going straight up to

the 38th

Parallel"

"A Korean babe stops me, and asks me if I could read her letter, and tell her what's in the letter

she

Holding in her hand."

"For me," she says, from the US."

I open it, and began

reading...

Mommy: "Ok! What did it say?"

Jonathan:"I quote ...!"

"I love you, my darling Kate! I know, we've got a 2 year old boy! I've reenlisted for another tour

of

Duty!

I'll                                     be with you, in a couple of weeks."

Then, I asked her about being called Kate.

She says: "One early morning, he suddenly got up and sang: "Kiss me Kate!"

"Now, I'm Kate!"

Kate says to me: "You know, when I was born, my parents called me Yoshiko. Then she said:

"follow me!

Let me take you to where I live, right now. And…, don't be critical!"

Well, we

Entered her room, with three tatamis, and a TORN U.S. flag thrown over them! "Don't be

disturbed by

The

                                                    Noises Next Door!"

She says.

Jonathan: "Please, lead me into temptation!"

Before we got in her place, outside, I read a watered-down sign:

                            Raise your Plow

                            Grand Opening

We entered her room, and sat down.

                            She offered me a cup of tea.

I heard loud noises from the other side of a thin wall.

Jonathan: "What's all that noise?"

Kate: "Go, and see for yourself."

Jonathan:"Ok! Ok! I'll go!"

I go, and walk into a room with a 60 inch TV

And, on the screen, a white girl,with her wide open legs,

With Tom and Jerry, holding them wide apart.

There's a message on the screen:

 "It's yours, for only US dollars, let's say $150.OO, for 2O minutes, and then the price goes up!"

I see her looking like one of our kidnapped secretaries!

My socialism pops up!

I find a heavy stick, and kill those 2 pimps! And I smash the TV screen!

Katy cries out: "They'll kill me!"

But, she kisses me, and she offers me a quicky, for nothing!

I repeat what my captain said:

"Gonnorhea!"

I say to her: "Why don't you wait for your husband?"

"That's my socialist upbringing, concerning a highly

Safe encounter with a Korean prostitute.

And…I saved the morale of the whole 8th US Army in Seoul."

Mommy: "You're like Tiresias! All the army's future in your voice!"

Claude Cahun, « Ecrits » (Jean Michel Place, 2002)

« Contre Attaque, Union de lutte des intellectuels révolutionnaires… » (p. 548)

"Who will I be, 10 years from now?"

Mommy: "I mean, really, really!"

"Besides,

She says: " I know you're a secret  admirer of Jacques Lacan! For you, is

He and…

"is" or has he become a "tomorrow"?"

Jonathan: "I heard my English teacher once say how Lacan questioned Foucault's

epistemology! He said,

During

Our break, in our 3rd floor corridor, he said, that, actually, there were no differences between

both of

Them

On Post-Modern art!"

The teacher was very earnest and, for our French education, he troubled us with a couple of

other

Famous intellectuals, especially Baudrillard, right now, touring US universities, with meetings, colloquia,

Invitations to lecture, and dinner, and here, right here, in a CUNY auditorium on 42nd street!"

Then he added:"Lyotard"

"By the way, mommy, both of them have terrible French accents, when they try to speak English!"

The basketball coach, dribbled in, saying:

"I'm sure students need to know English literature and English

History and English art." He underlined the stupidity of analyzing a poem, by asking a whole class to

Come up with their own interpretations of the same sonnet!

'Guess what: every student came up with a different interpretation, except for a Saussurian slant. And, perhaps a

Freudian one, learned in another lit. class."

The whole class broke out in hysterical laughter, and, nearly all of us, said:

"TO HELLL WITH THEORY!"

All our profs. knew,

We had them by the testicles!

History guffawed.

English smirked.

Philosophy smiled and asked what about Arabic philosophy, like Molla Sadrā?

I heard an elderly auditor, in Philosophy, say: "None of you can actually explain anything with your

Philosophy theories without coming up with Trotsky's approach! Otherwise, literature would soon

Implode, like capitalism."

And then, he added:" And don't allude to Alfred Jarry! Or the primacy of

Language, or your subway ideas on literature!"

Philosophy stuttered:

"Why not real works of the mind, and of the heart?"

Jonathan: "Mommy, I know you've been reading the "Second Sex." Remember, both Marx and Engels

Have

A section on: "Women in Greece, according to Ancient writers."

"Do as the Greeks do!"

Mommy: "Stop reading my memory! Remember what I was reading, 20 years ago! Besides, Jonathan, I

Know all about Elaine in the staircase!

And, Elaine's parents,

Squirming during the dress rehearsal of:

"Ballad for Americans."

Did they ever

Did they ever imagine what you were doing, on that third floor, with Elaine, or was it with June? I

Hear you sigh, when

You

Quoted "War and Peace," as if that work doubled another reality! They could, actually, see you walking

Down West End Avenue all alone!"

They said: "Do not stretch our imagination!"

They guessed you would go

To a 47th street porn movie! Then, they saw you enter a porn shop. They saw you flipping through an

Array of

Magazines, All with only women, old and new!

They imagined that, one day, you would step on the platform of Town Hall, and preach a revolutionary

Future to high school students!

They heard the applause.

They looked at each other, and said: "What

Kind of Marxist shit is he giving them?  Is it like an after- dinner mint?"

During all that imaginary time, Papa was reading the Forward's English edition. He knew Isaac's brother

Was a better writer! He knew that every word he was reading was the Truth, the Whole Truth and

Nothing…!

He knew Columbia was an uptown university, right in the heart of Harlem. He

Thought about his son. Wasn't it horrible to see him go up there? He talked about that danger to his…

Mommy said: "Shatzy: Cut all of that fear business!"

Papa: "I've just passed my "Bangladeshi grammar test!" Then he added, "All I have to do, now, is to go

On, for my Ph.D in that geography, then I'll be able to help all those Carmels!"

Mommy:

"Now, you're a Real Revolutionary!"

Papa: "I think that's what our son should have become!"

Mommy:" He's in Seoul, doing his job as a revolutionary."

Papa: "Stop jolting your memory! We're not there, yet!"

Mommy: "He told me what he had done, to save the moral values of 8th US Army."

Papa: "How, back then, I dreamt of a swimming pool next door!"

Mommy: "You see, you're not as pure a committed theoretician, as I once had thought!"

Jonathan breaks in: "Papa: Now that you're here, did you ever have a desire to go see a baseball game at

Yankee

Stadium?"

Papa answers: "That's for a bourgeois audience! And, besides, as far as I know, they've never had a

Black player!"

Mommy :"Why? Don't you remember that debate, at the Theater for Ideas: "when…"

Papa: "No! Don't bring in all that intellectual stuff, right out of a recent closet! Besides, she was a

Terribly rich widow…"

Mommy: "First, let me tell you a smelly story! We wanted to give our son piano

lessons, and so, we found a Bulgarian teacher, off Central Park, close to the Walden School.

Our son quickly came back, and he said:

"She stinks of garlic underarm smells!"

Anne Sexton:"The Complete Poems" (Boston: Houghton Mifflin, 1982.):

The boys and girls are one tonight,

They unbutton blouses

They unzip flies.   (p. 199)

Jonathan said: It's all Over! I can't stand sitting next to that garlic!"

Papa: "So we sent him to our friends, the Pintos, and Naomi gave him piano lessons, at least for a short

While!"

Mommy: "About…Yes, I'll tell you!"

She continues: "Don't leave out anything! Promise?"

"It all started when we got off the boat. We held on to our beaten- up luggage. Then, a hugely

Well-dressed man, looking just like a CAPITALIST

Approached us.

He said he'd

Give us enough cash to pay our rent, for all of next year!

He said his daughter wasn't in the best

Condition, I mean, mentally, otherwise, she's a fine girl! "Would you…

Could you convince your daughter

To come with me to Oregon, as a baby sitter? We live on a huge farm with bisons and

horses, and, everything you need to eat, at least for a whole year! You can see mountains in the

distance. We have a small pond where you can swim, in the summer, and, where you can go

fishing!

In our

Village,

Every Sunday morning, we get dressed, and we drive to church. Our neighbors are

Great! We

Help each other, in times of need.

They help us, when we need them!

How does all of that sound? Your

Daughter will have a beautiful room, all by herself, and a toilet, all by herself!

She'll eat with us, and… with our daughter!

She'll be part of the family and, every Sunday, I promise, she'll call you, or vice versa! If you

want to see

Her, I can arrange, that, too! We've got a small airport, twenty miles away!"

Mommy: (says to herself, and then, asks Papa),

"What do you think about all of that future for our Daughter?"

Papa answers: "You decide."

Mommy: "Thanks for all your advice!"

Robert  Creeley, "A Day Book". (NY. Charles Scribner's Books 1972)

Time to go

Back where you

Where going

Papa whispers: "Really, it's beyond my brain! Isn't it like selling your daughter to some Arab potentate?"

The well-dressed banker says: "Should I give you some privacy?"

Mommy: "I'm ready. Papa, are you? "

Papa: "Whatever you say!"

Mommy:"Somebody's knocking at our door. You get it!"

Papa: "You first!"

Katia reenters.

Mommy:"Wow! Are you getting married?"

Katia: "Maman, if I can call you that! You guessed it! But later!"

Mommy: "Where did you get that name? I mean, Katia?"

Katia answers: "When I was born, papa said I looked great! Maman then said, "let's call her

Catherine-

The-Great! "A couple of weeks later, they dropped the "Great!" And then, and there, I became

Katia!"

Mommy:"How you're going to pay for all of that wedding stuff? Besides, where did you get

that St

Petersburg look?"

Katia:"I'll pay with my Easter egg, the smallest one, where I hid my mother's gold, wedding

ring."

Mommy: "Tell me all about it! I'm dying of knowing!"

Katia: "One day, on Orchard, I saw a little sign saying, Mrs. Goldstone, Seamstress! I walked

up three

Flights of stairs.

I rang the door bell.

She answered.

I told her what I wanted, and I said I had my mother's gold

Ring,

And, would she do me a beautiful blouse, just like the ones they wear in St. Petersburg, for

Great

Events!"

196

Mommy :"You sold your mother's ring for a blouse?"

Katia:"I did! You said, you wanted to know everything!"

Mommy:"What did you say?"

Katia: "I told her, I don't have a blouse to change in, ever since I got to America!"

Mrs. Goldstone: "Ok! I measure you!  You something material and I make blouse for you!"

Katia:"I did what she told me to do!"

Mrs. Goldstone said: "You smelly your arm!  Oy! Vat a smell! vash in the kitchen, with kitchen

Towel! And, no use much water! What

Material do you want…?

Don't use lots of soap. Don't…"

Katia:"It was

Winter cold!"

Mrs. Goldstone: "What you want?"

Katia: "The most expensive blouse, if you want my gold ring!"

Mrs. Goldstone: "Do you hear my son, Bernie, pushing at the door? Coming in, dis minute! Please, open Door!"

Katia: "But, I'm wearing nothing on top!"

Mrs. Goldstone: "It's OK! He see lots of "it!"

Katia:" Ok. I'll let him in!"

Bernie enters

"Wow!"

Katia :"Should I go and hide, behind that curtain?"

Mrs. Goldstone: "Go!"

Bernie: "Top or, well, both? It reminds me of a cookie I loved when I was a kid! Vanilla, for the top,

 Chocolate for the bottom!"

Mrs. Goldstone says to her son: "You smelly your arm! You up and down Allen Street? Go to kitchen,

Take towel. Wash!"

Bernie: "Remember, mommy, I told you, Jonathan is coming over, almost now!"

There's a knock at the door, and Jonathan walks in.

"Mommy, do you want tea?"

(Turns to Katia)

"And you?"

(Jonathan can't keep his eyes off her.)

Mrs. Goldstone: "Don't stare!"

He stares, as if he had never seen a half-naked model!

"WOW!"

Bernie:" I learned this, in my Freshmen English:

Robert HERRICK

She has virgins many,

  Fresh and fair,

Yet you ate

More sweet than any…

That's it!"

Jonathan: says:                              "You made my day!"

Here's mine, from Michael Faraday!"

Do not conceal those

Breasts of thine

More snow-white than the Apennine

Bernie: "Not bad! Not bad at all!"

"While we're at it, here's my last, from Shelley:

"I arise from dreams of thee

In the first sweet of night

Katia says: "Look at him! He's staring straight at me!"

Mrs. Goldstone: "A College memory! Ok. I got measurements! You come in three days."

Katia looks at Bernie's friend.

Bernie says:" I'll go down first! The two of you follow! (He sings…)

Katia starts to walks down the steps.

Slips.

Jonathan's there!

He catches her in his arms!

Jonathan: "Now, can we go for some tea, maybe, a little pastry? I know a pastry shop, right around the…"

Katia: "Just, this one time, because …because of you, I have two legs!"

Mommy: "That was your foist date! Then, he wants see you again!…and again!! You said: Ok!"

Katia: "You're a mind reader! That's the way it really was, and then, three months later, he asked

Me, if I wanted to marry him." I said:

"Yes!"

I said "Yes" once more.

We kissed, for the very first time.

Mommy: "When's the wedding? It's   a…   TRADITION!"

Katia: "As soon as Mrs. Goldstone finishes my blouse and… skirt, and then, I'll really look like

a bride

From St. Petersburg!!"

At home, Mommy hears a knock at the door.

Papa says: "I'll do it, this time!"

Katia walks in (Again)

Mommy: "When you must go, in the middle of the night, please don't flush! It makes too

much.

Noise, and, then, your father wakes up, and mumbles to himself: " I can't go back to sleep!" He

hums

A worker's song.

There's a terrible smell.

She asks: "what is it?"

"When he was young, my son had a sleep-over and…well, that's it! I tell him, make your bed.

This ain't no hotel!"

Katia undresses.

Slips on her night gown.

Goes to the kitchen.

Broom in hand.

Brooms the kitchen floor.

Papa: "I'd call the NKVD, if he doesn't stop doing that! He'll make his bed! Or else!"

Katia:"You'll be my mother and father for the wedding!"

Mommy:"It's Sunday! We call her, in two minutes!"

"My Daughter…"

Over the phone, she says: "About my charge:  She cried all night! I got into bed with her, and calmed

Her down. We

Talked and talked about the "Wizard of Oz," and she melodied Judy Garland! For breakfast, we had

Scrambled, with sweet potatoes!"

Julia Kristeva ,"Histoires d'amour" (Paris: Denoël, 1983)

«Aussi loin que je me rappelle mes amours, il m'est

difficile d'en parler." (p. 9)

"She loves me!"

"Mommy, you'd love the countryside, all

around here, and the hundreds and hundreds of bisons in the fields! And the small pond, where we can

Dip in, when the sun's out! Her father drives us to church, every Sunday, and when it's finished, we go to

The drugstore and, just like in a painting, all of us sit at the counter, and all of us have a chocolate

Malted. With all the other kids in the village, we sip the same thing, with long straws."

The family says: "We love you!"


Papa: (whispers): "Sometimes, I wish we hadn't given her away,

For a

Fist-full of dollars!

Soon, it'll be her birthday.

What to give her?"

Mommy finished the last chapter of "The Heart of Darkness."

Then, she's begins George F. Kenan's "Siberia and the Exile System."

Papa says he thinks he knew a Minor, who had been sent there, to the salt mines. By chance, he

Had read a copy of his manuscript: "Memories of a Soldier of the Revolution."

There, Minor described what it was like to dig out the salt and, that horrible food he had to eat, every

Morning, around 5' o'clock in the morning, he says, somewhere, how disgusting, especially for

me, the

Son of a

Bourgeois Family!"

Next Sunday, same time, she said how much she misses all of us!

Mommy: (She hands the phone over to Papa, and tells him not to speak for too long.)

Papa: "Just wanted to tell you how I miss you!"

"First, and I never told you…

Terry Eagleton, "Criticism and Ideology, A study in Marxist Theory."

(London: Verso Editions, 1976.)

"The relation between text and ideology then…" (p. 100)

" When I first saw you,

in your crib,

 I had high hopes of enrolling at St. Petersburg U. But…I soon found out, no Jew could get in!

That didn't stop me from reading my favorite writer and, in one of his stories, a Horse did the

Narration!"

"Wow!"

Mommy: "You know, in my case, when I was very young, I loved Pushkin, who begat Gogol

and Dosto…

Later, I learned they were all canned by the Soviets, or so I heard."

There, in front of her floor-to-ceiling mirror, she measures me!

There I was! In my brazier!

Allen Ginsberg," Kadish

and Other Poems, 1958-1960" (San Francisco: City Lights Books 1961.)

with your eyes

with your eyes of Russia

with your eyes of no money     (p. 34)

Mrs. Goldstone says good-by to the three of them, but before Katia and Johnathan leave, she

gives

Them a bit of good news!   She tells them, her best friend, a couple of years ago, gave birth to

Identical twins! She gave birth to identical twins!"

She said:"I named them both: "Jonathan." Not the First, nor the Second, and that's

Because… But at the beginning, she told me, she named one: "One" and the second one:"Two."

But then "One" became Two and "Two" became One!"

And then, she paused, and added:

"They look exactly alike.

They talkalikytheywalkalike

When one fails,

The other takes over.

They tell each other all about their love lives or, should I say, their love life!

That way, if one leaves the country, the other one steps in, without hesitation!

If one were to have an accident, the same other would take over!

So far

Not a single girlfriend has

Ever noticed the difference:

There ain't one!

One dreams.

So does the other,

And it's always the same dream.

Once, I whispered to myself, if one were to die, I'd dream of having the funeral out in Sag Harbor, a

Plot not too far from Yerushalmi's.

I promised myself, I would really weep!

Katia: "Can't you really tell them apart?"

Mommy: "It's a secret! But for you, my future Daughter-in-Law, here's the truth! Both shave every

Saturday morning.

By Wednesday, one's clean, but the other one, he has hair coming out of his left nostril!

That's the TRUTH! I kid you not (you like my new American?)

(In the meantime, Jonathan stares at your barely baby body's breasts!)

Katia: "When she's finished, I get dressed."

Bernie says:  "He'll be the first one to go down the stairs: You follow me!"

Slowly, I walk down the stairs, from the third floor

To the front door. Jonathan does the same, in front of me.

Then, I slip,

I thought I'd break my back.

Jonathan saves me, in his arms.

"How would I like a hot cup of Russian tea and…some Russian pastry, right around the corner!"

Could he see me, that night? I said 'yes' to the man who had caught me in his arms! I'd be without legs if

He hadn't…

That was our first date.

We began, seriously, to date! After three weeks of drinking hot tea together, he looked very

serious

And he asked me, if I wanted to marry him!

"Yes!" (I said, modestly!)

"He kissed me on the mouth!"

Papa: "After learning all that stuff, didn't he say he would arrange your honeymoon on some

desert

Island?"

"Yes! He asked all our friends, and all of Mrs. Goldstone's, to get us as much money together,

to

Make sure he would get a proper honeymoon!"

"Both of us got bushels of wrinkled dollar bills!"

Jonathan      went to a local travel

Agent, and got us two round-trip tickets to Antigua. The dates were fixed: Arrival: Saturday

morning.

Leave

Friday at 10 o'clock.

"Why?'

"They've got to clean up, after us, to get the place ready for Saturday!'

Katia, and her future husband, jumped into a Continental, out of Newark, going to Antigua. They

Kissed

Crazily, all the way, before landing in St. Johns airport.

There, they jumped into a taxi and said:

"Please, take us to Antigua Village, please!"

He drove us through a herd of goats, on the road!

Once at the Village, we put on sneakers, and started walking, from Coconut Grove, the

Restaurant, right

On the beach, to the end restaurant, across Halcyon Village. There, we kissed, voluminously!

That night we decided to do that very same walk, this time, past Sandal's late night noise-makers!

The sea had landed lots of pebbles on the beach.

Further on,

The sea had vomited triangular bunches of seaweeds.

Jonathan had been waiting, for that moment, so he took off his blue jeans, and, all that was left, were his

Very tight black jockeys, made in China.

She followed suite.

Both left their jeans, folded over the first rung of the life guard stand.

He looked like…well:

She read: «Défense de toucher!»

Marcel Duchamp and Enrico Donati.

From the back, it looked like she wore a two piece bathing suit, probably bought in some magazine, Perhaps, if

She could recall,

On p. 28.

In the sea, for the first time, both his hands touched her, way down below!

Her hands did the same.

Then, back to their love secrets. And .saw, as a wedding gift from the boss, a large basket with a

large local fruits, and a note:

"Have a Great Life, Together!"

That night, they yelled.

They began:

Humpingpumpingscreaminghurtingpuffing

(Just like they do, in Swedish movies.)

They made so much coordinated noises that, 23A called Security, in the middle of the night, to ask them

To dispatch a guard, and go knock at their door, and tell them to be quieter!

Jason did just that, and, for a time, they imagined he'd be back in the Security Booth, and tell Wilson,

The other night watchman, what he had just done!

Next day, Josh got them a local taxi, parked in front of the front desk, and asked if they wanted the

Driver to drive

Us to the Epicurean Market.

Somebody, at the moment,

Told them to get some food and

Lots of bottled water!

Off they

went.

They told Wilson to pick them up, an hour later.

They pushed their way through innumerable aisles,

Buying too much, but having lots of fun, beginning with a baguette, some cold cuts, a bottle of rum,

And 10 bottles of Wadddadly beer!

Princeton UP, 2008.  "Selected Poems of Solomon Ibn Gabirol"

But I'll tell you something I've heard

And let you on it dwell on its strangeness (p.28)

That night, seated in front of their huge TV screen, they saw a basketball game.

She had never seen a

Basketball game before.

 They stayed there, seated, his hand on her right lap, to the end, when U. Con ferociously beat

Florida,

63  to …he had forgotten,

 With all that smooching, during the break when,

They ate a huge amount of pop-corn, SHE INSISTED ON CRAFTPOPCORN and,

While, we're at it, he said:

"No chicken fingers for me! Think of all those poor amputated chickens!"

For the first time, they drank lots of Waddadly beer!

The next project, Joshua had in mind, was a visit to St. Johns.

Wilson took them there.

The minute they got out of the taxi, 10 guys, all holding maps of the island, offered trips around the

Island!

"No!" They said!

They walked down Market Street.

Beautiful jewelry stores.

Katia said they didn't have any money, except for food, ice cream and taxis.

They sat at an outdoor ice cream joint, and saw the arrival of the largest ship they'd ever seen!

Somebody, next to them, said:

"3000 tourists, on that ship."

Then another, of the same size, parked next to the first!

Joshua loved to drive.

He rented a car, in the parking lot, outside the Reception Desk, and drove off.

He knew how to drive in

The States, but here, those damn Brits! They all drove on the wrong side of the road! He said it, until a

Car

Smashed into us.

He was instantaneously turned into what he would have loved best: a traditional pastrami sandwich!

She was saved.

She crawled out of the front seat, crying very loudly!

She carelessly looked at him, and she saw hair growing out of his left nostril.

At home, they arranged a nice burial, in a wooden coffin.

And, after that, everybody came back home, and stuffed themselves on deli. Rye bread and

fried

Artichokes, a straight out recipe of a Kosher restaurant in Rome.

When Katia spoke about all their experiences, she cried, and she wept.

Mommy (to change the subject) said it was very possible that her family came from Segovia

Before…and she stopped, to gather in her breath, and then she said: "all that before… before

the

Inquisition. She

Said, and then, she forgot. Then it all came back,

With a touch of pride, she said she might have been a descendant of Julio Chacon, a

descendant of Arias

Davila.

Could she remember all of her past? Or was it, probably, silenced?

Mommy looked around, and looked straight into Johnny's eyes.

"You must go to Antigua and recover his body."

Katia: "How could you tell them apart? You said they were identical twins? Does that really mean, they

Were one, and shared every, but every experience they ever had? (except, of course, the hair growing

Out of

His left nostril!

Mommy: "I can't help it, but I can't forget their college pasts! When the time came to go to college: one

Johnathan, went to CUNY. The other went to

Columbia.

CUNY identified all the lefties, in the Thirties, who became big deal critics, writers for Partisan Review

And, in many, many, other places! Lots and lots became high school teachers.

Columbia's Sociology, assigned Jonathan a paper on CC in the 30's.

He went back to the 30's Columbia Spectator, to read who had written some of those lefty articles.

There, he found Chambers, and his friend Zukofsky, both of them, with almost commie views, as far as

Senator McCarthy was concerned.

Zuk wrote about a new barrage in the Soviet Union.

Johnny came back, with what remained of his CC brother.

Johnny: "You'll never guess what I found in Johnny's inside left pocket, in his Burberry jacket! Just

Like mine ! »

"I'll give you

Three guesses…"

Mommy: "Two tickets for a Columbia football game!"

Johnny: "No!"

Mommy: "Ok. Stop with the jokes. What you found in his left pocket?  Let me ask you a small

Question: he wearing, what underneath, I mean, where his belt… Was it a

CalvinKleinaTommyHilfiger. A Ralph Laurens?"

(Which I had bought for the two of you!)

Johnny: "I found a hand-written sentence he had copied from Marx's "On the Jewish Question." I copied

That

Crumbled-up text!

Here goes, mommy:

"Religious ideas will finally evaporate only when we have put an end to the atomism of society and

Chased away the fear and the anxiety, caused by the rule of money."

Then, the following quote:

("We no

Longer see religion as the basis, but simply as a phenomenon of secular narrowness.")

Then he further copied …

"Therefore, the state can have emancipated itself from religion even if the

Overwhelming majority does not cease to be religious in private."

Finally, let me add, If Mommy wants to

Learn more, let her read: "Marx for Beginners," Rius, p. 18.

Then, he added, in his own secret code, we

Had made up, when we were seventeen. Next to Marx, our alphabetical bookshelf, after Marx,
Henry

Miller's "Tropique de Capricorn." (Translated from the American. And sold in French, under
the counter,

At

Shakespeare and

Cie.

He quoted one of his passages, in English: "True, he had a greater grasp

Of Reality than other men.”

Mommy: “You know, Jonathan always wanted to be a writer, but he couldn’t make up his mind,

Whether

 To imitate one of his Columbia profs, who did lots of writing in sociology, from a Marxist

Point of view?”

HE ALSO BOUGHT LOTS AND LOTS OF BOOKS AT Strand’s,

( ..............                            All on Political Theory.  He alphabetized all of them …)

And, squished them into our narrow bookshelves.

Mommy and Katia cried.

Especially Katia, who had grown up in the Soviet Union.

She asked for a box

of Kleenex.

The funeral was a religious one, in Sag Harbor.

Then, all went back to Aunt Margie, who had prepared little sandwiches, lots of tea and

cookies.

Later, Daddy barged in: (he couldn’t help it…) How he would have wanted a diploma from St.

Petersburg

University, but he … got it into his head, to check out his ancestors. Now, a word about anyone of his

Ancestors, and, both of their large families, all in all, at least 5 or was it 6 children?

Back in Russia, after a pogrom. (He remembered *Isaac Babel's stories.*)

But he didn't stay long. .His family jumped into a small bus, and, a day later, found themselves

at a

Harbor

Where they

Paid (lots of money)… to take them

To Ellis Island and then to Manhattan.

Ellis Island… There, they opened their mouths. They looked into our eyes.

And So on and So on… and on.

Once they got to New York, close to all those buildings, they felt all looked like huge banks or

Cathedrals, like the ones in St. Petersburg!

They talked to their children, because…they knew Katia was doubly pregnant!

What had really happened?

Much later, well, one day later,

Out of politeness, later on, Katia went back to Mrs. Goldstone, to thank her for

That blouse.

Then, she remembered how                                    She fell down the stairs.

She slipped.

She slipped.

                    Johnathan caught her in his arms.

(I wondered, what's the function of repetition in a novel?)


Later, she wondered

                    Which Jonathan?

                            By now, she knew both of them were

so  so much Alike!

They walked to a close-by pastry shop, for cookies and tea.

They got along so well, so they decided to get married! But, then, she said:

"Maybe, I'm going too fast!"

Everything went so fast!  Really fast, our honeymoon was planned for Antigua! Then, well, the car

Smashing up.

(NY:SUNY Press, 2001)                              Douglas Robinson, "Who

Translates?" "The (ideo) logic of spectrality" (p. 116)

"I'll spare you the bedroom details, but those couple of nights, before the car crashed, were

great!"

Once a month,

                        Both received, from Oregon, a heavy envelope, with cash for the rent.

The same ritual, every Sunday.

And, that ritual phone call!

They talked and talked!

                        That previous Sunday, she said the girl she lived with, and took

Care of, was a troubled girl, about her own age. She said, I give her pills twice a day, three, in

the

Morning, before breakfast, and three, before going to bed. They seemed to work. She would

Momentarily

Calm down.

I'd turn off the lights, before going to bed. Sometimes, in her dreams, she would say, she fell

Off her bed and cried out, on the floor.

 She says she's got bugs all over her body. She says she can hardly

Breathe.

I got to take care of her, every time she's in trouble. Sometimes, I thought of making my own

Dish, for an appetizer. My mother taught me how to grate beets, same for carrots.

Sometimes, I also made potato salad, with red onions, and all of that, drowned in Italian Virgin Olive Oil!

Then,

She'd

Ask me what I did the whole day! I had already told her what I did, probably twenty times before!

Where did we live? Did I have a large family, with lots and lots of cousins? I tried to teach her how to

Sing the Star Spangled Banner, but she refused the National Anthem, for reasons I was never able to find

Out.

She asked me what was my preferred book?  I said, Guy de Maupassant's necklace story, or even

Dickens' "Hard Times."

Every Sunday, when we leave Church, somebody, of her own age, says to her: "read Mark Twain, the

Greatest!

And Victor Hugo's poem, on his drowned daughter."

She cried, when she heard me read an American translation. Then, she'd ask me, if I had ever eaten a

Bison steak?

She wanted to know if my family went to church, and wore crosses.

Her father promised that both of us would go on spring vacation, like all the other kids in

town.

                         In her daddy's brand new Chevrolet station wagon, with all those

bright colored Wood all around it!!

She asked me if, coming from the old country,

Did all of us bleach our brown hair, blond??  She had seen it on a TV replay program.

I said: "A Crazy woman I once had met, changed the color of her hair once a week, from

brown to yellow! She

Had to

                    Do that, otherwise, she said, the brown would pop up!

                              One day, I spotted

Blood on her sheets.

                              She yelled.

                                        She wept.

                    She walked around, like a crazy person!

I took out a red magic marker

From her play box,

                                     And painted over all that blood.

She laughed, and, like me, did the same thing to total her sheet.

You could see, she had talent!

                                                  The whole bed

turned red!

Then, both of us ripped up our sheets.

                            We cried.

We laughed.

I did that, to comfort her, and she cried again, maybe, to comfort me?

When her mother came in, by chance, she hugged her daughter, and told her, there was

nothing wrong,

And that, as of now, she was a woman!

Her daddy, who would always like to change the subject, during dinner, said he would vote

Republican, because they wanted to abolish abortions, and refuse to allow gay marriages. He

really

Thought North Korea should be atomed, before they bombed our United States of America.

Daddy looked at me, and said I was the nicest girl he'd ever met, with the

Exception of his own daughter.

He thanked his good heart, for having helped my family get out of being thrown out in the
street.

They did find an apartment, near her newly-made friend, the Sterns, at 34 Hester, near
Orchard.

I told him my parents said he was the kindest person they had ever met.

(I wondered what had he done to make my parents so sure of his kindness?)

At home, my daddy once told me, when his son came home, he dropped his things on his
bed…and,

He yelled out: "Who cleaned up my room?" (In his heart of hearts, he thought he might have
been taken

Away

By the NKVD, and wind up in some Siberian salt mine.)

Mommy and Daddy knew perfectly well that he had never made his bed, that he always threw
his

Clothing, anywhere. That his closet looked like a museum exhibit, from some sort of a wild
tribe! And,

when he was slightly younger, he'd have two or three sleep-overs. In the morning, you might
think this

was part of a Soviet propaganda demo. of U.S. capitalism! It really smelled…

That following Sunday, Katia said how she washed her young protégé's hair!

                                    Both sang some songs they

Had memorized.

She dried her hair with a large yellow towel.

I dried her body, and she asked me to do it all over and over again! She said it really felt great!
It took

Me

                                        The next bath to realize what she really meant!

            Ludwig Wittgenstein, "The Blue and Brown Books" (NY: Harper Colophon
Books, 1958)

  "A gives B an order, consisting of one symbol, a geometrical figure painted in a particular
colour…"

(p.84)

Her daddy said he would not join a group of patriots, who worked out in the nearby forest,
firing their

Beautiful Russian-made rifles, at make-believe Mexican immigrants!

He had met the boss, and had congratulated him, but he told

Him

He'd never shoot an animal, running, in the forest.

Daddy said our country was menaced by all those gays, free-thinkers, feminists, in fact, all those who

wished to keep their guns at home, even though, in the next village, a 14 year old boy had

found his

Father's hunting rifle, in the garage, and shot his high school teacher, because she had given

him a B- on

His mid-term exam!

To fill up the void, after all those violent discussions, I showed her how to make a Heart for

Valentine

And draw sweet things, for mommy and daddy, for their birthdays.

I tickled her, as she always wanted me to do, especially when she got out of her bath, and

especially, when she climbed into bed.

I scratched her back, when she was in bed.

Once, she told me, she wanted to soap me, once I got into the bathtub.

                                        She loved

Soaping me.

                                                                She loved it,

When she dried me, with a huge yellow towel.

All that, on Sunday mornings, before my call to my parents!

When church services were over, the preacher stood on the outside steps, and shook hands with

Everybody.

But one day, she told me,

She could only dream of imitating a Morandi she had seen, in some magazine, probably in a
Sunday art

Section in the

NY Times.

She painted bottle after bottle, and glued them all over the house!

 I understood she loved to paint, if I did the same. So, I did my Andy Warhol.

If it weren't for me, she'd have no friend, no one who would come over to play with her.

They must all have weird memories of her, in school, before she was asked to leave.

In the family, we were the only ones to know she lived in a world totally of gauze.

When her mind stumbled, we thought she might be having a fit!

When Daddy heard her, twisting on the floor, her eyes red, her mouth twisted, he figured he
had never

Told her about his military service, in Korea, close to the 38th parallel, where, once, he thinks,
he had

Seen the

Very same thing.

When it started snowing, I told her how to make a snowman, and stick a carrot in its face.

I taught her how to make a snowball and throw it at…well, at the front door!

She laughed, when she saw her snowball stick to the front door!

Once, when she happened to walk into her daddy's work room, where she found a funny magazine on

His work table.

A girl, with a man, both naked, playing games with each another. She never thought that a man

Could play that way.

She took off her clothing and, staring at herself, on the floor to ceiling mirror, in her parents' bedroom,

She tried to imitate what she had seen

All by herself.

She cried with pain

And pleasure,

Then, she fell,

Nearly fainting, on her parents' bed.

For her birthday, her father gave her a bathing suit.

He said, if she wanted to, she could roll down the straps.

Her mother, on the other hand, said she had to keep the straps on or, they might fall and, and there she

Would be…well, she made herself quite clear!

When we had no plans, she loved to sit in front of the family's TV set, and switch channels, even though,

She said to me, she had a hard time looking at French movie titles, way below!

She said that, to her daddy.

He said they would go see an eye doctor.

The following day, he drove her to the next town.

The doctor gave her drops to put in each eye.

A while later, he did say that, six months from that, she had to return.

"Maybe,

Cataracts?"

One day, when she got tired of not seeing the titles on some T.V. show, she decided, without thinking of

it, to raid her daddy's book cases. There, she found, by total chance, alphabetically, an illustrated

Surrealist catalog. She told me, she really hadn't the slightest idea what all those pictures were about,

But they were really hot stuff.

                        For the next couple of days, both of us drew what

we had seen.

We signed our names, on the right hand bottom.

We dreamt that, one day, our work would be, in one of those pages, even though, in that

catalog, there

Were so many, many names, she had never heard of before.

She was particularly hypnotized by naked kids, and naked women, she found in Kenneth

Clarke's NUDE

And then,

                        She mimed Max Ernst.

She thought Salvador fabulous, especially when he painted a naked, bent watch, like a

woman's

Body!

She shivered,

When she admired Man Ray's iron, with nails on its back. Torture seemed to be ā la mode,

In that catalog, and, she asked me,

"How did he plan to use that iron?  Could he have had the nutty idea of

                        Scratching a

woman's back?"

But, most of all, she was totally taken by Hans Bellmer's bikes, with women, shot from behind, and

Doing

Something, in a plate, and, all of that, with his camera, and for our pleasure!

Turning the pages of her daddy's surrealist catalog, once again, she returned to Kenneth Clarke's NUDE,

Where

She found an extraordinary source of pleasure for

Her hand, her imagination and, all that, she drew, with a pencil, on endless yellow legal-size paper.

I quickly understood that, if she couldn't listen or work, or read her class assignments, I realized it all

Came

Down to a simple fact: Nothing, really, captivated her imagination, however I tried to follow her father's

Instructions.

No reactions on her part!

(Gérard Genette, « Mimologiques, Voyage en Cratylie » (Paris : Seuil, 1976.)

L a.  L aa. [an. [aa.  (P. 114)

"You can't possibly imagine her joy, and her quick pencil, when she turned a page and saw those

Naked cupids, in Ingres' 'Venus," or those two baby nudes in Carrevagio's "Danaë." All in Kenneth Clark.

My first Sunday, when I spoke to my mother, my father and my brother, that first Sunday, I told

Them how amazed I was to see how she could concentrate, with her new vision! What a talent!

She spent so much time, imitating painters!

Then, she turned to me, and said:

"Could I ever get into one of those catalogs?"

She turned, once again, to that catalog, and continued painting, almost blindly.

I had never seen her smile,                                                    so intently

When she finished her daily work-out, as she called it, when she put all of her drawings together, took

Some Christmas wrapping paper, and folded her work in it.

She asked me to print her name.

She said this was the best adventure of her life.

From now on, she told me, she'd raid her father's bookshelves.

She whispered to me that, for her next birthday, she really wanted a Picabia!

She forgot, as soon as possible, both the magazine and the catalog, and her father's silk smoking jacket.

She didn't know it, but I knew she was a budding painter and, if she continued, I'd ask Mommy to find

Her all the needed equipment and…when she had had photographs taken of her work, Mommy

Promised to walk up and down Madison Avenue, Chelsea, and the Lower East Side, to enter every

Gallery, and, ask them what they thought of her work.

She did just that.

She went to see and talk to the famous ones:

BrookeAlexander Paula

CooperGladstonNancyHoffmanKraushaaPeterBlumMarianGoodmanHirschl &

Adler,

And, smaller galleries, only opened from Wednesday through Sunday:

The Artist's InstitJack, Hanley, Gallery

Pocket, Utopia

Mommy, with her pictures, went everywhere:

                              "No!"

                                     "No!"

                                            "No!"

She could have gone on and on!

Did she ever suspect that, as soon as Melody (the name I had given her, since she was able to

imitate

Everything she had ever heard!) became her real name, came to

New York.

She'd become the darling of TV interviewers' passions!

All the galleries she had visited, now

Wanted to meet her, and shake her hands.

                                                                 I said to

them:

"Don't tire her out! Try asking her short questions and, I think, she'll be able to answer!"

                    Die Zeit L'observatoreLa RepublicaLe MondeShogummyDailyWorker

And, in Russian, PRAVDA,                                        Means: "TRUTH"

"I'll answer their questions, as fast as they come!"

Simone de Beauvoir says, convincingly: "women are not born..."

"Please, look at my baby nudes."

She said they were all in her dreams.

"Think of those male desires… Nudes, I think, function as a referential system, founded on

Acknowledged, or not, anterior lives, dressed or undressed, as in my nudes."

"Yes?"

"Creation as an anterior presence, therefore…"

"To each man, a hint of

his sexualities."

Christa Wolf: "Aucun Lieu. Nulle part." (Paris: P.O.L.Hachette, 1979)

"Et aucun juge. Aucun juge."  (P. 17)

She says: "I really believe art is distant from

memory."

 "My nudes are hints of my future! Now, my nudes, as a beginning of life, out of their cradles,

endlessly

Rocking!"

Hummy (that was my make-up name) throws out a possible reference: "Her father's

bookshelf."

No! She doesn't read! She works, while her father hums: "Ballad for Americans," a communist

musical

He says.

Now, journalists left Melody alone We ate, for breakfast, poached eggs, on buttered whole wheat,

Toast.

I decided, right then and there, to fight the salt industry. "Salt is evil for your Health!"

I was arrested for blocking traffic, and illegally handing out my mini-manifestos.

I spent a night in jail, with drug addicts, who were regularly beaten.

Then, a school friend of mine…

Now, a well-established lawyer, got into the act and got me out!

Now, I think I knew a little bit more about my grandfather's life, at least in Siberia, as his bio. told me!

"Why Melody?" My father asked me…

"When we heard the "Beatles,"she'd  melody."

"She did the same, every time I played a Sinatra, a Crosby, the Beetles, and Lady Gaga, eating doritos.

She mimicked all those melodies.

She became Melody, but she already had that name!

I became Hummy! That's all I could do!

"Let me tell you"…and her mother and father said:" she couldn't handle her school work."

                              She hated to be told what to do. I already saw her, one

afternoon,

Pencil in hand, imitating those naked women.

Then, one night, in the middle of that night, I rolled out of bed.

                              There she was,

Holding my hand,

Helping me climb back in bed.

She melodied one of the songs we both had listened to.




                              The Others

                    The Others

                    The Others

                    The Others

(You wait…)

(Waiting)

She kissed me.

                              She tucked me in.

Somehow, for a tight little moment, time had reversed itself.

She had become me.

My mother, finally, found a gallery, right in the heart of Chelsea: The Thomas Jaeckel Gallery. Up one

Flight of stairs. Turn right. There, great white walls!

He said: "I'd like to see her work! Could she come see me, in the gallery, when she's in town?"

I flipped.

She had no idea that her life drawings would catch anyone's interest!

"Only, Nudes!" She'd say, modestly.

"That's all!"

Her father and mother were stunned.

Both reeled.

They looked at her, as if she had never existed, especially, as a desired painter of nudes!

They looked at me, as if I was the one who had done all that work for their daughter.

"Really,

What are we supposed to do, with all that filthy stuff?

What the hell will our neighbors say?"

I popped in: "I'm sure mother and father would put up sheets, on the couch, in the living room, where

All

Our things are piled up! And then she could sleep right there!"

I called.

My family was stunned: "What are you saying? Who's the girl?"

Her mother and father, Melody and me—we all took a plane to Newark and then, by Carmel,

To our new apartment, on Allen Street!

The first visit to a huge gallery came early next day.

He said: "Show me your work!"

She took out her drawings.

He clapped.

"Who's your teacher?"

I'll skip over all the other galleries!

Thomas Jaeckel signed her up for her first one man show.

The New York Times' art reporter, relished in her work.

"Amazing," she wrote.

"Melody's not quite 13, and, here she is, a fabulous artist!"

TV interviews followed.

The least fascinating, for Melody, was Charlie Tulip. He surrounded her with art critics who could only

Speak of the young painters they had known, and that they knew right now, right out of the crib. "You're

13: HERE'S THE LATEST LIST OF THOSE PAPERS, INTERESTED IN INTERVIEWING YOU:

Die ZeilL'observateurLa RepublicaManchester GuardianLe MondeShumgummyDailyWorkerPravda

Other interviews followed, and, actually, they couldn't make heads or tails of her talents.

"What's your next project, I mean, after all those curvy drawn, painted, or stolen?"

By that time Thomas Jaeckel had sold all her work.

Her father said: "She's got to have a lawyer. He'd be there, when she signs her next contract."

Her father switched out of his daughter's fabulous successes.

He wanted to tell his daughter, and me, how he had gotten that silk smoking jacket, made in Hong Kong. He

Talked about Hiroshima.

He said, how fondly he remembered a young guide he had gotten at the JTB=The Japanese Tourist

Bureau! A shapely, Esther Williams type, in her 1 piece bathing suit, a Japanese silk suit.

Then, I could imagine my daughter, out there, in the fields, or swimming in the pond, behind our house.

He would never have imagined, that, one day, she'd become rich, and a celebrity, in New York! The very

Idea

Would never have crossed his mind! But, there she was, signing and selling all her work! He could hear

Voices in the gallery, asking Jaeckel to bring out more of her nudes. They went so fast!

Later, that night, or in those very early hours, when the sun rises, he'd pull out one of his nudy

Magazines, and

Caress himself, until he splattered semen, on the left side of the bed, while his wife slept on the right.

His daughter never suspected a thing.

If she couldn't deal with her homework, even her friend, sent from New York, she would soon find out,

She

Was a white piece of paper, waiting, just waiting for a nude!

She'd be her best friend, forever.

She'd never had dreamt that, one day, totally ignorant of literature and history, she'd be a star!

Her father said: "What will she do with all that money?"

I seem to have heard all that before, just like her father's memory.

She was my age.

I wanted her to do her homework.

Impossible! We were

inseparable.

In one of the recording studios, I was asked: "what was my name?" I said: "Hummy!"

Then, the photo shoots.

Rockefeller Center.Central Park ice-skating rink.

Virginia Woolf, "Orlando" (NY: A Signet Classic p. 1960)

"As this pause was of extreme significance in his history…" (p. 50)

She rode a rented blue bike,

Along

A path, on Riverside Drive.

On the ferry boat, looking at the Statue of Liberty!

Then, and maybe, then, they'd ask her, at least for that moment,

To walk on the Washington Bridge.

She tripped

"Does it hurt?"

"The Complete Poems of Anna Akhmatova" (Boston: Zephyr Press, 1992)

"I didn't laugh, and didn't sing,. I kept silent all day…" (p.481)

Mommy could hardly talk.

I had an eerie feeling that the past wanted to return, as an adult wants to return to his distant

past.

She would never have said her father had said all of that, before.

 She heard him say, as she thought it was a perfect reel, run backwards, how much he would

have

Preferred skiing in Oregon, rather than in Utah.

Was it all a translation of the past into the present? Did he bypass his own nudity

problems? I Heard

Him repeat and repeat, as if, what he said, took time to come up to the surface of his feelings…

then, he

Seemed aware of what was happening, that is, all of those moments, in Tokyo with a JTB.

A complex translation.

He wondered, out-loud, if anyone could hear him, and then he decided to correct his

thoughts, saying,

                                                                    "Damn my

memory!"

Inside, somewhere in his head, he heard a critical voice: "Yours is not an accurate translation!"

I remembered, T.S. Eliot, writing, in "Murder in the Cathedral," that the body of St. Thomas

had been

"Translated" from Canterberry to London.

It's all a question of accents.

Private words left out,

Words censured,

Ready to correct the translation!

                              But, what about the Truth?

"So, what about it?"

He ignored, or cast aside, as not proper in a translation, if it was meant to be read/heard by

Somebody else?

And by whom?

He let a type of censor intervene.

Then words, he didn't ever think of, might come out, would ever come

Out.

That made him pervious to his past:

He refused to talk about his daughter.

 Somebody had

Moved his nude magazine, to the left,

Where he had placed it, inside his drawer.

Or, was that another rejection of a mistranslation?

Really, wasn't …

He was in touch with his alphabetical mind?

He scratched his head, where he thought that everything on his book shelves had been misplaced by

Only one

Surrealist catalog, not only by another, but next to that, a copy of Bataille's work.

And, then, again, without looking up his "B" section, he checked out Realism, in order to justify his

Theory that REALISM had been dramatically discarded by SUR---

He flipped through his dog-eared B's, and he saw why the Surrealists so admired him. He thought Breton

Had, in a manner of fact, digested Bataille's "l'Erotisme," and that, he had also read Desnos, Aragon,

Artaud…

And, next to that, he knew Breton had, hand-written, Lautréamont's "Les chants de

Maldoror."

He could no longer believe his own doubts.

Was it all a mistranslation of some "Truth" without a referent?

Then, he hummed:

"Ballad for Americans."

Why did he split out of translation?

Now, and without conviction, he imagined his daughter, scanning somebody else's daughter,

maybe, on

An ice skating rink?

This time, he seemed to be sure that, what he was looking at, was actually the Truth!

He saw, she saw a girl doing twists, and turns, on the ice skating ring, in Rockefeller Center.

She heard her mother suggest that the three of us could go skiing, not far from home.

Melody believed the girls, who were twisting all around, were robots, something she knew

haunted her in

The

Rink or, at home, in the bedroom of her mind!

"Who are those robots?"

In her dreams, or so, she dreamed, she had seen those same robots, all

Around her, attacking, like mosquitos, biting her body, all over her body.

She quizzed herself: "where did they come from?"

Would somebody have mesmerized them, and directed them toward her sleeping body?

"Why"?

 She wondered, was her mind playing tricks, or was she having one of her recurring

nightmares?

She wondered where all those games came from?

I showed her how to correct her work, on the computer and, especially, how to delete things

she

Didn't want to

Keep.

She asked herself, was there a way she could auto-hypnotize herself?

Could a computer double her brain?

Edmund Wilson, "To the Finland Station" (NY: A Doubleday

Anchor Book) (1963).

"We have seen such late French historians as Michelet, Renan, Taine, how this rhetoric…"

And then, if she didn't concentrate, could she eliminate those robots, Those mosquitos?

Nobody could ever have suspected she lived both within, and outside, of her dream realities.

Nobody, not even in her dreams, could she, alone, make those dreams come true, as if she could or, kill

Them, like a great white whale.

She had rejected all forms of education, because she knew she had another way of learning chance,

That was her best source of information, but dreams were much more seductive.

If she thought about what she had learned, about translation, she asked herself, if, by that technic,

She could push up those dreams, right up front in her mind, or find a way of transferring what was in the

Back, to what should be in the front, to encourage them to pop up?

Somewhere, way in the troubled front of her memory, dreams seemed to perculate.

Did they all have the same identity?

"Could I have-- she said-- could those dream ribbons of thought-- bring them to the surface of my

Consciousness?...

Beware

Beware

Beware

Beware

Beware

Just bide your time

To my awareness?

Perhaps, memory itself was an icon of the past? Or did those dreams

Dream something, like closing doors, then opening them up again?

If dreams were encircled, could they be kept at an unknown distance?

Masked dreams? (Ain't

they all?)

Reality, a distant procession of a future landscape?

I refused to turn around in bed.

In bed, at that non-hour, at least an hour I couldn't imagine, I thought dreams were skip

roping or, were

They encircled by other dreams?

I said to myself, if only dreams could get out of their grooves, as a needle, out of an old

fashioned

Record player?

I so wanted to be able to translate them, from an unnamed past, into my eyes, so that I could

see them!

I saw a metaphor: if I tried hard enough to dig into my dreams, would I reach them in secret

archives?

Or, were they hidden behind all of papa's books?

All those hours, before the sun came out, and lit the world!

Maybe my search could end with light?

Somebody, within me, said to me, perhaps she'd invented all those dreams, so precious, at one

Moment:                                                                          Cleaned them out of the next?

I said, out loud:

"Don't leave me alone!"

I got out of bed, and came to hers

To calm her down.

She asked me if I was I having a

Nightmare? One of those recurring ones…

(I asked myself, was I part of her nightmares?)

I held her tight.

When she turned around, in her sleep, she mumbled something like:

A while later, I thought the best way of getting those nightmares out of reach, and see them

fade,

Beyond

Recognition, was to read her some of my favorite poetry, like Novalis, Oppen, and, one of my

really

Favorite ones: Shmuel Ha Nagid!

THE GOOD STUDENT TENDS

The good students tend

To doubt mysteries;

The foolish—what's obvious.

And the skillful singer

From the well of reason

Draws wonder on the rope of his hunch.

I thought you might like that one! It's short, and, perhaps…yes… makes you wonder!

She said she liked what I liked, but what really made an impression on her eyes, was the cover

of "The

Yellow Submarine."

In the meantime, in another bed, she could hear her daddy make funny noises.

He cried:

"There are no more cries, anywhere."

Then, the phone rang.

The bell rang four times. (Could it have been the postman?) (Does it mean you've stopped, or are going

To Stop, just like the bell for air-

Raids in school?)

Paris : Editions Circé.  Alexandre Pouchkin : « Rousselan et Ludmila" (1999)

«Et il s'arrête, le cœur battant au moindre craquement du parquet." (p. 121)

Then

A  Choice

Made

(Please, do not lose all hope…)

Then

it stopped.

We had done our recording:

"Please, leave a message for Melody or her family. We'll call you right back. Thank you for your

Patience!"

Mommy heard her dream-nightmare, and called our family doctor.

He drove through the most recent snow fall.

"Tell me, where does it hurt?"

(I didn't want to tell him-- it was all a fiction, a dream turned into a nightmare, where I couldn't tell the

Truth!)

He left

Gave Mommy a couple of pills, and said:

"Three twice a day!"

And then, he whispered in her ear: "If that

Doesn't work, Call me."

As he was about to leave, he did turn around, and answered her muted question:" I'm off to Acres

To buy a coffin."

(They say, he didn't suffer much. He did say, so they said, he said: "Fairfield."
We all knew

That was our cemetery.)

That afternoon, I read an article on amnesia.

"O" I said to myself, maybe all that dream stuff, all those recurring nightmares, they were all a way of

Shunting aside memory?"

She jumped up

On the left side of her bed, and started counting: "One bison, two bisons, three…"

She thought she had heard her father promise her she'd have her own bedroom in the Sleepy Hollow

Motel, when Easter Vacation came around.

I once had been there.

I could remember those blue birds flying on flowery curtains.

The hearse drove by our lane.

"How did all that happen, so fast?"

"Well, even the doctor didn't seem to know!"

I borrowed mommy's black raincoat.

It was very, very cold outside.

Richard Wright , "Native Son" (NY: Harper& Row. 1940)

"You make it alright?"

"Yessum."

"You see her down there?"

"No'm."

(p. 116)

The coffin was lowered into a hole.

Somebody said:

"He was the kindest man I ever knew!"

Somebody else, murmured: "Did anyone call his son?"

A couple of tears.

Five wreaths.

"Not many," I said to myself.

Lots of pictures taken

Then, all of us drove down to Hester's house.

She had prepared little sandwiches, tea and coffee.

That Sunday, the phone rang, again.

Mother picked it up: "Yes, she's right here! It's your mother!"

"Hello mom!"

Her mother:"I told our friends you've been working, as a  part-time baby sitter, out there,

Somewhere in Oregon."

Her mother added: "When you get back home, you'll go and visit all our friends! They've been

asking for

You!

All of them want to kiss you!"

I landed in Newark.

My parents were there.

A Carmel waited for us.

They paid for it, took us home. (The price, the voice said: "$65.00 plus toll & tip."

"Your parents are the kindest we've ever heard!"

She got out of Carmel and, there they were: her parents, and all

Our friends, right there, with two bouquets of yellowing roses.

A neighbor said: "Boy, she's really a grown-up little girl!"

Another one, noticed she'd put on a couple of pounds.

Our neighbor, on the second floor, was thinking to herself:

"Now, she's really a

chubby one!"

In her first Sunday Times, by chance, she turned to the matrimonials.

All those photographed couples!

She whispered to herself: "I'll cut them all out and draw them all out with my hand!"

(A saxophone under the following observations)

AGES at death:

| SHE | HE |
|---|---|
| 72 | |
| | 69 |
| 77 | 81 |
| 83 | 73 |
| 99 | 83 |
| 92 | 79 |
| 99 | 84 |

If they didn't tell me how old they were, at death's door, they did tell me the dates of their births.

(Now, a clarinet solo)

How old where the bride and the groom?

| 32 | 41 |
|---|---|

32                                          42

32                                          28

28                                          43


The article when on to print where they had gone to school. Diplomas. A nice

Photograph of the couple: Girls and Boys and Boys and Boys

(We had to guess how much it cost the parents, for that wedding

Reception!)

Where the marriage had taken place:

They'd be a half a page photograph of some fancy hotel dining room with palm trees, like the

Chinese

Waldorf.  Or the Botanical Garden.  Or, on a famous TV producer's  farm, totally remade, with

5 horses in

The stable.

One group was driven, in a horse-and buggy carriage, to the deserted Grossinger's.

The bride wore a beaded bolero over a fit-and-flare gown.

What they were doing now: he was an associate in some

Accountant's firm. Another one was a senior on the board of a public relations firm.

Another one was a deputy director in an advertisement firm, still, another was on paternity

leave…

(My parents told me they knew he was, really, an editor at the Forward.)

(They wrote that, in secret, in law school, he found pleasure in drinking a priceless French

wine from

Burgundy.)

NAMES

| SHE | HE |
|-----|-----|
| Sarah | Charles |
| Pat | Joseph |
| Rachel | Thomas |
| Leila | Andrew |

The now-bride said, she

Would keep her maiden name.

The photograph, on the left, said his grand-parents had founded a Lower East Side Deli, which

they had

Founded,

At the time, when Russian Jews had to come to New York.

On the right, his father was a doctor in Newark, and

His mother, a lower school psychologist, in the Bronx.

His father was a chemist

His mother: a stay-at-home

A solo tenor


Sometimes, the article mentioned the fact that the groom's parents had emigrated from the

Soviet

Union.

After a powerful rain, some of the writings on old tombstones were barely visible.

Somebody had scratched, on a family grave, in Woodstock: "Pravda."


It turned out, her mother came from Moscow. She had gotten her advanced degree from Lenin

U.

They celebrated all

Jewish holidays.

Then, out of curiosity, since she had never had the Sunday Times, in Oregon, she checked out

the

Fashion

Section.

Albert Camus, "The First Man" (NY: Random House, 1995)

"Providing musical commentary to the news" (p.95)

"Wow!"

"Who would ever wear such under where?"

"I want to go swimming! Maybe at Jones Beach !"

She said: "I want to buy a sexy bathing suit, one of those featured

in the New York Times' Sunday, Style Section."

(You could almost hear her dreaming, out-loud.)

She was quoted as saying: "Right there, on a Sunday beach, I saw the cutest young man, in a

tight black

Bathing suits".

Things went very fast.

He swam over.

Smiled.

"Well, you can guess the rest!"

"He saved me from drowning!"

The article said, she nearly died, slipping on a sandy crevice!

Well, the rest, is family history, and, somehow, she said "yes."

They held hands. (Somebody had taken their picture, right on that beach.)

A quote: "He said the water might be shark-infested."

Now, she remembered her own life's experiences.

His arm went around my waist.

Afterwards, both of us walked on the boardwalk.

Ate hot dogs.

Drank cans of coke.

Out of the blues, he looked at me, seriously, and, in a whispering voice, asked me if we could take a little

Walk downtown.

"Really!"

I said to myself, will this be like one of those pictures I had seen in some of my father's magazines?

"There's a small hotel!" (He hummed.)

We kissed in room 38.

Then, she switched from the article to her own life.

That was really my first, with somebody's tongue in my mouth!

We took off our bathing suits.

We jumped on the double bed, thick cover and all!

Bounced!

He closed the
curtains.

I could only think about what he had in mind.

I had seen all that magazine stuff, in the left hand drawer, of my papa's chest of drawers.

I really didn't know how to call it, but, there it was, nearly lost in a bushel of reddish-brown
hair. And it

Looked long and very fat, like a German hot dog!

I felt my nipples hardening.

It hurt.

"A movie?"

"Hope it didn't hurt too much?"

Blood on the sheet, like it had appeared, when I
was a baby.

He said: "I've dreamt about this moment all my life!"

I didn't want to add, but that, also, had been a secret dream of my own!

He turned around, junked the pillow on the floor, and told me his secret desire was to have
three kids.

Then we heard "Don Giovani."

(I had never given it a thought, I mean, kids!

Maybe in a dream?)

I whispered:

"First star I see tonight, I wish I may, I wish I might…"

He said he was the oldest in the family.

We went right into my dream.

I wanted to buy an apartment, on the Upper West Side, not too far from a good public school!
And, if

Possible, views on the Hudson River!

In any case, mother insisted we have sunlight in our bedroom.

Father said, he'd put down the payment.

We checked out the Times, and found out Bloomi's was having a furniture sale.

Once we got there, too many young girls were handing out sample perfumes.

But, boy!  We did buy a double bed!

We did buy thick yellow bath towels. (See above for the definition of those towels.)

Mommy said we had a lovely tan.

She said: "When the time comes, I still have lots of baby clothing, stashed away."

All she had to do was raid the back closets!

She was dreaming! One day, she'd become a grandmother!

She'd be taking the kids to a Riverside playground, roughly, opposite 84street!

She'd talk to other mothers.

She'd exchange joys and difficulties.

She added:"If it's a boy, blue!"

'If it's a girl, pink!"

I whispered to myself, all those antebellum thoughts!

"I'll buy the crib!"

Both of them, said:

"Both of us want to do some shopping for our future grandchildren!"

Daddy said he'd buy a "Sweeeedish Baby" stroller!  And, baby toys, so that the baby would become very

Smart!

And, when they finish high school, where would they go?

Mommy said she went to Barnard.

Daddy said his grades hadn't been so hot, so he enrolled in a CUNY Program.

He said: "You could dream Harvard or any other Ivy… You'd be with rich kids! (And a couple of

Scholarship girls!) Do you know how much it

Costs to get dressed for all those occasions?"

Mommy broke in: "If she's an athlete, she might try out for the swim team or tennis!"

Papa: "What's your dream major, in the future?"

"I want to major in French and comp lit."

He said: "I want to major in economics and then graduate, and, go work on Wall Street."

Mommy: "How about a dash of Russian, like a semester? I mean, one day, maybe, you'll travel
to St.

Petersburg, and visit the Hermitage!  And, maybe, maybe, you'd find the street where

We lived!"

Sunday, at three o'clock, I called Melody to give her the latest hot news!

"Hey, Melody! Great News: A full column, in the Sunday Times Art section, written by their
best, I mean

Robert Jones!"

Louis Zukofsky, "A" (Berkeley: University of
California Press, 1978)

"A round of fiddles playing Bach." (p. 1)

He wrote, and I'll quote:

"If she's 13 now! What can we expect

When she'll turn fourteen?"

I could see Melody, dreaming of being fourteen!

When I left her, standing there, she must have thought how sad she would be, without me! But then,

She'd hide under her bed and, with her blue pencil, draw a nude!

He suggested his son should go to Ramaz.

She suggested it was best for the family to let her decide, all by herself, after having visited a number of

East Side Privates, where they all wore blue uniforms, played field hockey, in the park, next to the 96th

Entrance. If any girl was hit by anything, the school had a resident doctor, and, if that didn't do the trick,

(Before her parents sued the school) she'd be escorted to Mt. Sinai, right around the corner.

But we lived on the Upper West Side.

All we had to do was to pay a foreign-speaking nanny to push our baby, in her beautiful, Swedish-made

Carriage!

Once a year, for her X-Mas vacation, we'd let her go home, to her family, on some Antillean island.

Daddy said: "I know, it's a bit too early, but I insist on giving her a private math tutor!"

Mommy said: "You're right! I'm thinking of that horrible core curriculum!"

Daddy: "Forget it! Our baby won't go to a public school!"

Mommy:"We'll pay Shimada, our cleaning woman, to show up, once a week!"

Daddy: "I know you've never given it a thought, but I'll pay Paquito to clean their windows!"

Hummy: "Now, here's the toughest question! What's going to be their names?"

Mommy: "How about my grandmother's?"

Daddy: "Why not Shmuel,  my grandfather?"

As time goes by

Melody said: "I had a dream!! We'll draw pick-up sticks, with all your family names!"

Daddy: "Sounds good!"

Hummy whispers: "Don't forget! Our parents invited us, this Friday, for din din!"

Mommy: "Can't I put in a modifier? I've changed my mind! How about Karina, for our granddaughter,

And

Howie, for our grandson?"

 Her husband said: "Sounds good!"

Hummy: "You know, when I took care of Melody, in one of her dreams, she popped up, right out of bed,

And yelled out: "Jenny!"

Then, she called out:

"Piotr!"

Daddy: "Where did she ever come up with that Russian name? Mellow, did you ever talk to her about

Where we come from?"

'We could not have found ten pages of possible names, for a girl or a boy! Maybe in the middle of the

Night.... "

Hummy: "I sent an e-mail to Melody, and here's her answer: two nudes—

A baby boy, in diapers

A baby girl, the same

And, a long list of boy's names and girl's:

| Boys | Girls |
|---|---|
| Craig | Betsy |
| Peter | Victoria |
| Aron | Stephanie |

| | |
|---|---|
| Justin | Deborah |
| Andrew or André | Sandra |
| Erin | Yvonne |
| Robert | Natasha |
| Norman | Michelle |
| Maurice | Katie |
| Morton | Marlene |
| Steven | Frances |
| Stan | Nancy |

She said: "Now, it's up to you!'

(Much too long!)

The family pondered:

Mommy:"How about…boychick?"

Daddy:"girlckick?"

"You can always make a baby room out of the servant's room, I mean, next to the kitchen! It's small, but

There's a faucet! And… a toilet!"

"She's not a maid!"

"He's not a delivery boy!"

"In any case, hang a Calder above the baby carriage!"

Hummy: "Let me call Melody, and thank her for her list! "

"Remember, when you took her father's rent money, I went to take care of her! Now, will she recognize

Me?  Maybe, in one of her long-lasting dreams, maybe, a dream she grabbed

on the run? I forgot to tell you, if you really want to give us a gift, how about a 40 inch flat TV screen?

Mommy searched, in an old handbag, and came out with a very old necklace, given her by her

grandmother, for her 16th birthday, in St.Petersburg!

"I want you to have it!"

Daddy went back to his tattered travel bag, and came up with a pair beautiful cuff links.

"It's for you,

From my grand- daddy."

Mommy: "She was lucky! Very lucky to have escaped the tzar's cavalry, chasing Jews all over

Odessa!"

Babel writes:

"Are they all dead, those Jews?

No! Not all of them."

Mommy and Daddy remembered, when they got to NY, a social worker was going to send them to the

Bronx. "You'll be with lots and lots of people just like

You!

A nearby, Yeshiva, and a kosher deli!"

Daddy: "When we moved in, we were on the 4th floor, with 5 trees in a small garden, below. To keep my

Mind working, I talked about Rousseau and Fourier and, closer to home, Pushkin and Gogol! I know you

Were too young to appreciate what grandfather had talked about in his Siberian salt mine!"

Mommy: "Stop!"

In the summer, we sang the "International!"

"What a song to hum! Even if we didn't believe a word of it!"

Daddy: "In synagogue, women take their ritual baths (with the hope nobody placed a camera to observe

their naked bodies!) And… don't forget what my father said:

"Always be a Jew, and you'll always be able to convince them, when you see them…well, you know

What…!"

Mommy: "Don't overdo all that stuff, about memory! One day, if you don't watch out, he'll

give you a lesson on the Kabbalah, and its symbolism!"

I jumped in: "Just look around," I said, smiling: "We're surrounded by Russian Jews, and, who

knows,

Some from Spain, talking Ladino!"

Bernie pops up:

"Genug ist genug!"

"But, if you're really interested in all that stuff, read Philip Birnbaum's "A Book of Jewish

Concepts."

Mommy: "Come on, all of you, sit down. it's a "simple," but I did it all by myself! No delivery

boy! No

Chinese noodles!  No wonton soup!"

Jonathan: "Let me give you a hand! When the time comes, I'll say the prayers."

Daddy: "By the way, Jonathan, I never did ask you what you do for a living?"


Jonathan: "Glad you asked, just to clear the deck, so to speak!  I' m an accountant in a big

accounting

firm, downtown, with lots and lots of offices, all around the globe! "

Daddy:                              "Then… No problems with the rent!"

Hummy: "Just read Melody's e-mail! She writes: 'I'm overjoyed, it's really over!!! I followed one of my

Hearing dreams, right down to my neighborhood arsenal. I got in, saw a hundred canons, all lined up, each one with

One of

my dreams! There they were, hiding all that time!  Were they all the same? Would there

Be a slight difference or, were they all the same variations, on the same theme, something which had

Haunted

Me

For all my nights."

                              I sat there.

Canons looking straight at me.

Seated on them, I saw hundreds and hundreds of little dream paintings. I was about to say:

                              Poems!

"Imagine me, all by myself, opening up my mouth, as if my dreams, all along, had been a form of food For

Me!

But they never looked at me!"

Hummy:"I've been doing some hard thinking, about you know what!  I read a "Tao Thought"
you might

Dig!

Washing at dawn:

Rinse away your dreams.

But protect your dreams

Within the gods within

"Here's another stream of thoughts!"

Theatre of Memory: The Plays of Kālidāsa (NY: Columbia UP,
1984)

"My mistress sends me to get a citron…" (p.274)

"Maybe your dreams are all rejected dreams! As if you were, once again, all alone, let's say, before
I

got to…"

"If I remember correctly, you gave each dream a name! Like Hamnet and

Judith!

They say, those were Shakespeare's kids!

276

But your quest might have been a fear of dreaming! Perhaps, a touch of melancholy! I

Know what you're thinking! Some of those dreams may have scuffled with other dreams!

You might be living an echo, where dreams actually dream!"

"Isn't it more important than the dream itself?"

Melody: "Well, I wish my parents had taken me to the movies! I think I might have taken all those

Images, with all those men, dancing, those women doing the same, with Fred Astaire! In the meantime, I

dreamt of baby nudies! Now, that I'm 13, maybe I'll always be 13! I mean, a prisoner of the Zenda

Of my dreams!"

Hummy:" Let's not push it!"

Jonathan: "We've eaten too many dreams! I'm getting sick and tired, right down to my stomach! But, I've

got to tell you that, in 1968, the University president, Kirk, phoned in for tsarist troops to "liberate"

Mathematics, taken over by students!"

Now, memories were taking over!"

Fall. 1968.

Students got together, and made up a new course on:  "The Urban Black Family."

"And… to justify that course, a complete restructuring of readings…"

At the same time, the war in Vietnam.

We screamed.

We sang.

We went to Washington,

We wrote

Poetry.

.Walter Lowenfels, poet and anthologist, put us all in "Where's Vietnam? American Poets

Respond: An anthology of New Works by 87 poets," published by Doubleday Anchor Original,

1967.

Here are two stanzas of my own:

Testimonies for a School Prayer

Now we are at peaceful war

Quickly the child ducks

Behind a kneeling cardboard tank

Shot up by paper planes

When I grow up

Torn from a box-top

I'll build a bomb

 Drop on cereal cities

. . . . . . . . . . . . . . . . . . . . . . . . . . . . . . . . . .

"Who were the other poets?

                              Dickey

                              Ferlinghetti

                              Ginsberg

                              Kunitz

                              Levertov

                                        "

(You can't imagine how thrilled I was to be in that family!)

Hummy: "I've been doing lots and lots of a retro type thinking about…your dreams!  if you were once all

alone in your

crib, surrounded by a nation of dreams, filled with discarded words, I'd say, your troubles might have

been reduced, had you written all of them down, on an invisible sheet of white paper! Then you'd

Become your

Own

Repetition!"

"Ok! Did you ever think you might be living an echo? Somewhere, where dreams are

Naked and so, it'd be … Tell me if I'm off by a thousand miles?"

Melody: "I'd really have been much happier had my parents taken me to the movies, every Saturday

Night!

Then, I could answer one of your hidden question, and I'd reply, that's the reason I draw all those naked

Babes! You should know better, I'm still a 13 year old, but now, we can't be separated! No division!"

"Who knows when I'll paint full bodies, so many of them, in pictures, I I'd love to sneak in Kenneth

Clark's NUDE!

Maman:" Who will say the prayer? "

"It's Friday!"

Jonathan:

"Me!"

Maman:" I didn't know you still knew how! You and your lovely chanting! You, wearing that

Berber

Yamulka! We'll listen to that beautiful music, from the mountains of Morocco!"


 Papa: "I'm getting hungry! By the way, you never did tell us what you do on Holy Days!"

Jonathan: "No, I don't go up to


Monsey,

for High Holidays, with fifteen pieces of luggage, stuffed in huge station wagon, with ten kids,

from my neighbor's apartment! That's only from the 2nd floor!"

Papa :"It's eleven o'clock! Let's see the awful news on channel 21!"

"Those massacres in ebola Africa!"

"That disease…"

Mary Ann Caws, "Provençal Cooking" (NY: Pegasus

Books, 2008)

"…At first, we felt alone here, surrounded by strangers, in a land strange to us." (p. 67)

"Don't tell me, it's all the fault of colonialism!"

Jonathan:"Who brought the chocolates? The fruit salad?"

Mommy: "Sit next to me, and I'll give you the best recipe for…"

Papa: "I hear, it's a joke? You're called Hummy! I don't know what the hell that means, but I do know

What we got here. Somebody told us, when you were young, to send you to: "Kinderacres." For your

summer vacation!

or was it :"Wonderworld"? I was told they had boys and girls. In the old 30's, it was a commie camp, and

they still hum the "International."

IMommy: "Bouby, I know you're only interested in Tolstoy, Jammed with all those French words!

But, please, remember Shakespeare!"

"As for me, I decided to read something more philosophical! Now, I'm reading Marx's "Les Lettres des

Classes en France (1848-1850)» I tell you, even in a French translation from the Russian, Marx writes

like hot stuff!"

Jonathan:"Before it's Saturday, I'd like you all to meet my friend, Roger. He's a Park Avenue psychiatrist

who

has not absolutely lost his German accent, but whose practice is highly…well, should I say, lucrative! His

Office is on Park Avenue. I did tell my Freudy psy. all about Melody's dream sequences.

His quick answer:

"Repressed: expressed!"

Then, he clarified his observations, citing Bergson, on laughter:

"When someone slips on a banana peel,

And falls,                                                  everyone laughs."

Melody concealed her daddy's penis.

Drew nudes,

Without any identifiable sex,

With her phallic pencil.

She knew she'd never model a clay nude! She said: "Too revealing!" That way, she brushed aside her

Creation.

"If      you      want      my      Park      Avenue      opinion,      viewers      love      the
sexless!      The      nudes      will      sell      like      hot      cakes!"      "Repressed…"
(THERE'S MORE HERE THAN MEETS THE MIND.)

Freudy writes to Melody: "Read Freud's "Totem and Taboo," translated by James Strachey.

"…a situation of emotional ambivalence." (p.49)

Jonathan turns to his future bride:"Sweetheart-my-soon-to-be-wife! I'm dreaming of our first night in

Bed, on our new Bloomy's double bed, built for a lifetime!"

Mommy: "Please, spare us the particulars!"

Papa: "I can see your new wife, hoisted up on your friends' arms, singing: "Hava Nagila Hava!" Followed

By a full-time reception."

Mommy: "I've reserved the third floor of the Columbia University Faculty dining room! Lots of

Delicacies, and lots, AND LOTS of deserts and wines, all from Israel!"

She added: "Honey, a wedding's a wedding!"

SHE     ADDED::     "Do     you     think     my     plans     are     a     bit     too     much?"

SHE     SAYS:     (again)     .:     "It's     not     for     us!     It's     for     family     and     friends!"

Papa: "Do you actually think we have that many friends, given that so many have moved

To an Elsewhere?"

She says: "Jonathan, you're an ambitious pervert!"

Jonathan:"I'm only thinking about our honeymoon!"

She     says:     "I     guess     I     know     what     you're     dreaming     of     doing,     on     your     first     night!"

Jonathan: "If you don't do it, I'll turn to the left and…well, you can guess!"

Next morning, they're in the shower, soaping each other.

She: "Do your parents have the slightest idea of your pervert mind and projects?"

Jonathan: "They once caught me, when I was twelve, wetting my bed. They said the sheets told them

everything."

"And they added: I shouldn't ever do that, ever again!"

She: "Anything you did in the normal column?"

Jonathan:"Did I ever tell you how I loved fancy cars, like the Green Hornet's? I also had a distant passion

for Lois Lane, and wished I had had some weirdo outfit to sweep her off her feet, and take her

To a phone booth!"

She:"Sex in a car?"

Jonathan:" Right on! And, how about you?"

She:"I've got to tell you about my latest reading: Georges Bataille's "Erotisme."

And…see Freeland's Film:"

"Nyphomaniac!"

"Sweetheart, you see,

You're                 not                 the                 only                 one                 with                 desires!"

Jonathan Swift, "Gulliver's Travels" (NY: The Modern Library, 1931)

"The reader may please to observe…" (p. 48)

Jonathan:"That's disgusting!"

Guy Debord, "The Society of the Spectacle". (NY: Zone Books, 1995).

"All the theoretical shortcomings of a scientific defense of proletarian revolution…" (p. 56)

The ceremony!

She: "How about Long Beach, where there's a little hotel? I could rent lots of triple sex, for our first

night!"

Mommy: "Think of that glorious day! Even though we got some socialist atheists in our St. Petersburg

Background, we were all accepted in Paris, before going to the Bronx! We left all our friends behind. I

later

heard they were all rounded up by the Paris police, and, trained out to Drancy, and then, to their deaths.

Papa: "Get to the point! Where's the wedding going to be?"

"You'll never guess it, I've reserved a couple of suites at the New Yorker Hotel, so our guests,

from

Everywhere, can get a

Hear of

Music from the Opera!

And when the hour arrives,

All of us will pack into old fashioned-limos and:

Are you ready for this momentous bit of truth?

The wedding will take place…

At the feet of

The Statue!

Of Liberty!"

Then, she added: "If it rains, there will be a huge plastic huppah, with a beautiful floor for us

to dance all

our traditional dances, and an orchestra, I rented from the Mannes School of Music! I've shipped

in

The Glucks, from Berlin, and the Noirs, from Paris, and lots and lots of our friends from the

Bronx and .... from

Florida! There will be a huge screen, so kids won't go bananas!"

Drinks for adults.

Sodas for kids.

We'll dance on an imported floor.

Our married couple will be the first ones!

A WALTZ!

And, just to make it religious, there will be a glass to be stomped on!

Wasn't that all a great idea?"

(Spare me the loud applause.)

"I love you all!"

THE END

"…and that's the Whole Truth, aint it ?"


ADD

Slavoj Zizek, "The Invisible Reminder"

"Incidentally, this surplus-enjoyment complicates the problem of…" (p. 93)

THE

End

**ROOTS & BRANCHES SERIES** TITLES ARE MADE POSSIBLE IN PART THROUGH THE GENEROUS CONTRIBUTIONS OF

Thaddeus Rutkowski
Lynzee
Lori J. Anderson-Moseman
Richard Martin
Lee Slonimsky
Elayna Browne
Kenneth B. Nemcosky
Barbara Henning
Katy Masuga
James A. Reiss
Elizabeth J. Coleman
K Feather Hastings
Susan Lewis
Michael Boughn
Karen Gunderson
William Luvaas
Stephen Sartarelli
Maximilian W. Valerio
Andrea Scrima
Lewis Warsh
Vitaly Chernetsky
Kathy Conde
j/j hastain
Andrew K Peterson
Marc Estrin
Gloria Frym
Dennis Barone
Marc Vincenz
Michael Forstrom